ACADEMY OF THE SERAPH

BOOK ONE

blessed

BOOK TWO

captured

BOOK THREE

broken

captured

academy of the seraph

BRANDI ELLEDGE

Printed by Ann James Publishing, December 2020
Copyright © Brandi Elledge, 2020
WWW.BRANDIELLEDGE.COM

Cover and interior design by We Got You Covered Book Design
WWW.WEGOTYOUCOVEREDBOOKDESIGN.COM

ISBN: 978-0-9967193-4-6

This one is for my Aunt B.

What makes a great aunt? Sassy, funny, and a little bit crazy.
And babe, you got them all.

I love you, BIG.

one

MY HEAD BOUNCED AND SWAYED with every step that my captor took. My mind was so foggy because, every time I would wake, I was immediately shot with a tranquilizer gun, over and over again.

When I woke this time, I let my body hang limp as Trev carried me over the rocky terrain. For whatever reason, I couldn't visit Finn in my dreams. Maybe because of the toxins running through my system. The moment I came awake, I tried to will myself to a peaceful sleep so I could talk with the one person I craved to see, but it was of no use. My mind refused to comply.

Trev laid me down in some sort of shallow cave, and as soon as he exited, I tried to get my limbs to work. I couldn't even feel my toes.

I lay there, unmoving, as he reentered, dropping a stack

1

of wood not too far from me. He was consumed with building a fire, and I was so consumed with trying to get my limbs to unfreeze that I didn't hear the other person come into the cave until he was upon us. I took deep breaths, pretending to still be asleep, if only to buy myself some time. Five minutes could be my salvation.

There was a light nudge to my ribs, and then a snarl.

My mind was foggy, but I still recognized Trev's voice. The traitor.

"Don't touch her again."

"Or what, little brother?"

Boots crushed the small pebbles that I lay on as someone paced in front of me. The same voice bit out, "What were you thinking of bringing her here? Why didn't you fly her back to the Empowered Academy? You do realize that being immortal doesn't mean that you can't die, correct? Thanks to the headmistress, she now has a way to kill the fully blessed. Granted, her weapon isn't as quick or as painless as the Flaming Sword, but dead is dead. After she injects you with the serum, she will tear your wings from your back then take your empty head from your shoulders."

Trev's voice was quiet, but there was steel laced in it when he said, "I'll tell you what I was thinking, or should I offer an apology for interrupting your whoring and drinking?"

"My patience is waning."

"I needed to buy time. I was hoping the headmistress would send you out for me."

"Why?"

"Obviously, because I need to talk with you. This girl is more than just a tool to lure the commander in. She could be our escape, too, brother. She could be the answer to a problem that we have been trying to solve for years."

The other man scoffed. "You always did have your head in the clouds, especially when it came to pretty women."

"Are you happy? Truly?" When Trev's brother didn't respond, he said, "This girl is more than just a pawn in a war. She can help us right our wrongs. What is the price you'd pay for freedom?"

"Who says I'm not enjoying life?" Even half-drugged, I could hear the lie in his voice.

"Do you realize how bad the Empowered Academy has become?"

The brother scoffed again. "No, I missed the selfishness and greed that has spread through it like a disease. I also missed the Satanic behavior. And let us not forget the dark magic, along with the makings of the wendigos. You say bad, brother? The academy passed bad decades ago."

"We can't leave," Trev said. "You know this. You bear the mark, just as I do. Not unless the first wendigo ever created is taken out."

"And you think that this slip of a girl is the answer to our prayers? That she will free us? That she will be able to take on a wendigo?"

"I would bet my life on it," Trev said.

"Well, good brother, because that is exactly what you would be doing. They sent me out to look for you so, in

3

all actuality, you would be betting both of our lives and anyone else who you bring into this mess."

I could feel someone crouching beside me.

"I sense a lot of power … more than should be possible." He leaned in closer to me. "She's waking. Her pulse is becoming erratic."

"So, do I dart her again?" Trev asked. "Or, do we have a deal?"

"*Again?* How many times can you dart someone who is mortal before they die?"

"Exactly," Trev said. "I'll tell you the rest once you agree that we have a deal. Are you in or out, brother?"

My eyes popped open to see a man in his early twenties peering down at me. He had hazel eyes and streaks of blond through brown hair that touched his shoulders. He was as handsome as his brother, the traitor, but he had a jaded look to him. Being in foster care so much, I knew his type well. The world had scorched him, and he still carried around the burn marks as a reminder.

"Please, no," I said. "No more darts."

He loomed over me. "Oh, and you think this beggar will be our leader?" He chuckled as he looked back over his shoulder.

Those extra minutes had given me enough time, as I was able to reach out and snag his arm. Remembering how I had killed using just my hands, I focused on the rage and fear I felt that night.

Trev flew to his brother's side, tackling him toward the

4

crackling fire. Their eyes were wide as they stared at me with … hope? Well, shit, that didn't go as planned.

"Did she almost kill me?" the angry Viking asked.

Trev smiled. "Yep. And I had to save your sorry ass. So, you know that theory you had earlier about how to kill an angel? Well, it looks like she carries the fast, more painless option."

A matching smile lit up on the Viking's face, and a dimple winked from under his left eye. Definitely siblings.

My throat was dry as I croaked out, "Smile now, you asshats, but when I get all my parts working, there is nowhere you two scumbucket pigs will be able to hide. I will find you, and I will kill you both."

The smile never dropped from the Viking's face as he said, "Such foul language. What's your name?"

My eyes were slits. "You can call me Executioner."

Curse words streamed out of the Viking's mouth, and then he patted his brother on the back. "I'm sorry I doubted you. I'm in. Definitely in."

Trev nodded at me. "If we don't show up with her, we're dead. We need a plan."

The brother groaned. "Savage killers? Yes. Witty banter with"—he gave me a wink—"devastatingly good looks? Yep. Making plans? No, we suck at that. All our plans always backfire."

"One thing is for certain," Trev said, "we can't bring her to the academy with all that juice flowing from her."

"Agreed."

Dodging my right arm, the brother crouched beside me. "What's the matter?" I snarled. "Are you scared, princess?"

The brother was laughing as his warm hands touched my head, and then pain like no other consumed me. My body bucked as something tight coiled around my head. My powers flared to life right before they puttered out like a wet blanket to a flame. I hissed as the pain caused me to bite my lip until blood pooled. Then everything went black again.

two

A COLD, CEMENT FLOOR WAS flush against my cheek. Not wanting anyone to realize that I was awake again, I tried to keep my heartbeat steady as I continued to take deep breaths. I didn't dare open my eyes. Not yet.

I tried to bring my powers to me, but ... nothing. It was as if I was human. I don't ever remember feeling like this, not even when I was a child.

"Are you going to lay there all day and pretend you're still asleep?"

I knew that jerk's voice.

My eyes flicked open to see Trev on the other side of steel bars.

Slowly sitting up, I took in my surroundings and laughed.

"What's so funny, beautiful?"

7

"You," I said. "You couldn't come up with anything more original than putting me in jail? Or, wait …" I patted the rock wall behind me as I stood. "Is this a dungeon? So much cooler, but still, you didn't really shock me."

He came closer to the bars. His brown eyes roamed over me like he was checking to see if I was in good shape. That was rich.

"Gabriella, we need to talk."

I waved my hand about. "Well, it looks like I have some time on my hands. But, for the life of me, I don't know if I can stomach looking at you." I slid down the rock wall with my eyes closed. My head was pounding, and the last thing I wanted to do was have a chitchat session with Trev.

Finn would come for me. This I was certain of.

A small smile curled my lips at the image of Finn storming into wherever the hell I currently was. I felt for our connection. He had bound me to him, and because of that bond, he would know exactly where I was. It was my only saving grace at this point.

I ran a hand over my chest. I felt … nothing. My eyes flew open and met Trev's. He winced.

"What have you done to me?" I asked as tears of frustration pooled in my eyes.

"I'm trying to protect you."

I made my way to my feet once again and crowded the steel bars. "Where am I? And what is your twisted plan this time?"

"I don't have a lot of time. I need you to listen carefully.

Everyone here must believe you are nothing more than a low-level demi. The headmistress of this school needs an object. An object that she has spent her entire life looking for. She believes that Finn knows where that object is. She also believes that you are the key to getting Finn to talk."

I narrowed my eyes. "Yeah? And how would this headmistress know that I might be the great bait for the mighty Finn?"

He gave me a sheepish look.

"You are truly un-freaking-believable."

"I know, and I'm sorry. I had to give her something—some sort of hope. Lives depended on it. I don't expect you to forgive me or even understand why I did what I did, but I am sorry. I did betray you, and the sorry truth is I would do it again and again if it meant saving the ones I love." He curled his hands around the bars that separated us. "I am trying to help you."

"I'm sure that there is something in it for you, though. I mean, excuse me if I'm wrong, but you don't seem like the unselfish type."

When he didn't say anything, I continued, "I overheard you and your brother. You said that someone had found a way to kill the fully blessed; strip them of their immortality. If that's the case, then why would this headmistress need the you-know-what?"

"Because she has to make the serum. I don't know how she does it yet, but I know that the source of the serum is limited. Also, there are steps she must take after she injects

9

the serum into the fully blessed. Then she has to strip the fully blessed of their wings. And finally, she takes their head. The other item that I was talking of"—he gave me a pointed look—"can kill a fully blessed or, as we know, an archangel within seconds. To have that kind of power—"

He stopped talking and put a finger to his lips before he pointed at the floor where I had been lying. Then he closed his eyes like he was sleeping.

I hesitated for a second before I went back to the corner of the small cell and lay down quietly. I didn't know why I trusted him, but I had nothing to lose at this point. The devil you knew and all that.

I took deep breaths, trying to even out my breathing as I closed my eyes, pretending to be asleep.

A few moments later, I heard heels clicking on the cement floor and a hand trailing along the bars, as if the person were taking a stroll in a park instead of walking in a moldy, windowless dungeon. I was more than tempted to peek through my lashes, but my instincts had me feigning sleep.

With a cold, feminine voice, the person said, "Hello, my pet."

"Headmistress." I had never heard Trev's voice sound so distant, so cold.

"Tell me," the woman all but purred, "what took you so long? My scouts reported that you should have arrived with the girl yesterday."

"Yes, but I thought we were being followed, so I chose to

stick to the ground, under the shelter of trees."

"Hmm," she said, "Wasn't that the point, though? To have the commander follow after the girl?"

"Yes, Headmistress, but I wasn't entirely sure that it was the commander who was following us."

"Explain." Her voice was laced with so much venom and ice that I was impressed with how Trev didn't waiver.

"I believe there are others who are interested in this girl for the same reason that you are."

"Camaella?" the woman asked.

I couldn't see what Trev did, but the woman then growled.

"Of course. That bitch would do anything to please Lucifer. She thinks she will get her hands on the Flaming Sword, but it is *I* who will wield it."

"Yes, Headmistress. That is why I took the extra day to get here. I was hoping to lead whoever it was following me astray. I knew it would be in your best interest to keep this girl, her identity, and what she means to the commander as quiet as possible."

"I took your word that he was enamored with the girl and would chase after her, but if you are wrong, I'll make an example out of you."

"Yes, ma'am. However, it doesn't look like I need to worry about that. Our scouts have located him."

"How many did he bring with him?"

"It's the commander we are talking about. Does it matter? I mean, his power is unfathomable."

The headmistress grunted. "So, he does hold affection for this one. That means he won't kill us if she is in danger. And you are sure she is a demi?"

"Very."

"So, no healing powers? How unfortunate for her. Take two and put them in a box. Tie it with a ribbon and leave a note saying he can storm the academy, but she'll be dead before he can reach her."

Two? Two what?

Trev cleared his throat. "As you wish."

They were both quiet for several seconds. Finally, the headmistress said, "He needs to know how serious I am about this. It seems that our commander has a decision to make. He can give up the whereabouts of the Flaming Sword, or he can have the girl. He can't have both."

The joke was on her. I was both. And if Finn wanted me, he would have both.

Energy hummed around me. Without my powers, I got no read on her, but something in me said she was testing Trev.

"Go get the items that you need for the commander's present and keep me informed."

I lay as still as possible as their footsteps grew farther and farther away. I was confused and tired. I had no powers, and I couldn't feel Finn, which meant he couldn't feel me either. Whatever Trev's brother had done to me left me vulnerable.

When Finn did show up, I would be absolutely no help

to him. We had so much to talk about.

A tear streaked down my dirty face. This couldn't be how our story ended.

three

THE AIR PRESSURE CHANGED AROUND me, giving a jolt to my system. I lay on the cold ground, but all of a sudden, I wasn't cold anymore.

Sitting up, I looked around me to see if I was alone. There was no one on this level, but I knew that someone was staring at me, even without my powers.

Four feet from me, a man appeared, but this wasn't any ordinary man. No, this was an angel, with brown, wavy hair to his chin and golden eyes that smiled upon me as if I was his long-lost daughter. All six feet of him crouched down so he could get a better look at me. His handsome face took in my features like he was committing them to memory.

The fact that I felt like a thousand suns were shining upon me gave me a clue to who this angel was. Plus, I remembered him from my last dream.

14

"Uriel?"

"Yes, it is I." He looked around at my surroundings. "I'd ask how you are doing, but I think I know the answer."

I scoffed. "Yeah, I've been better. Am I dreaming?"

He shook his head.

"So … um … my only memories come to me in dreams. I thought you had died."

"We don't really die, but if the Flaming Sword strikes us, then we are grounded to wherever we are meant to be. For some of us, that is heaven; and for others, that is hell. Once we are sent there by the Flaming Sword, we are not to leave. Of course, the Flaming Sword was never meant for the archangels, but rules are rules."

I squinted like I was prone to do when someone made zero sense. "Okay, so how are you here, then?"

"I'm not really." He cut his hand down toward his thigh like an axe chopping wood. His hand went through his leg. His whole body was blurry for a few seconds before it settled back like congealed Jell-O. "I have special permission to come visit you. Your mother sends you a bushel of hugs, by the way."

My eyes started to tear up at just the mention of her. "She couldn't come …" I waved my hand at him. "Even in that form?"

"No, I'm afraid not. The reason why is because we only have an allotted amount of time before anyone notices we are missing, and Abbadona knew that she would likely go over that time, and then she would be punished. Everyone

15

has a soft spot for your mother, so we all try to protect her when we can. Speaking of time, I'm cutting it close, so let me get to the point. Sometimes, what the heart wants and needs are two different things. I need you to remember that when your friend comes tomorrow. Make a choice that your heart can live with."

"Wait—who are we talking about? Finn?"

"You'll see. Now, to the important part. The blade that Azrael poured into you is no longer meant for one person. If you are to defeat the fallen and their creations, you will need people around you who can help. Seven should carry its essence, including yourself. Choose wisely."

"Creations? You mean us?"

"Things that should not have been created." He stood up.

"Wait," I said. "No offense, but you can't just drop in here … a cell of all places, and tell me that I need to pass the torch to six other people. I need details, like who and how. Also, let's talk about these creations."

He smiled. Like freaking smiled as if he didn't know that I was aggravated.

I made it to my feet and stared at him until he spoke.

"I've been touched by the Flaming Sword. I can't alter the future. I'm already treading into the danger zone, and I never said *pass the torch*. You will still be just as powerful. Each day, you grow more and more powerful." He reached out a hand like he was going to touch me, but his fingers disappeared the moment they should have come into contact with my cheek. His eyes grew sad. "I must go. Your

16

mother is probably pacing the floors right now, wanting to know every little detail of our exchange."

Another lump formed. "Tell her I remember her, and she was a great mother."

He frowned a little. "She still is. Just because she is in heaven and you roam the earth doesn't mean that she has stopped thinking or caring about you."

I didn't know what to say, so I just nodded.

"Abbadona is signaling to me that time is up, so I must go."

"Wait!" I shouted. "How will I know who to choose?"

"You will feel it in your gut. Let Chamuel's gift guide you. Whomever you pick will be bound to you for as long as you walk on this earth. You will all share a common goal. And remember, you can't make the best choices if you live in safety. We are all rooting for you."

I watched as he literally evaporated in front of my eyes. Then I paced the floors of my small containment.

Uriel was cryptic; that was for sure. You would think he would have given me a little more information or help in the matter. Shoot, why not just give me a list of names of who could be trusted?

The good news was that he didn't seem to think I would waste away in this cell.

I went back to lying on the floor. I knew sleep for me was a lost cause, but while I was waiting for my gut to lead me, I could hope to fall asleep and dream of my mother or the boy I was missing.

four

BEFORE SLEEP COULD TAKE ME away from this hellhole, an unwanted visitor came back seconds after Uriel had left.

I narrowed my eyes. "Tell me exactly what the headmistress meant by *take two*. And I swear to you right now, if I don't like the answer, I'll make sure you die a slow, painful death."

Trev looked exhausted. "Two fingers."

"You have got to be kidding me."

"I wish I were. I had a feeling this would happen."

I stood. "You had a feeling that some psychotic woman was going to demand a part of my body?"

He sighed heavily. "I knew that she wasn't going to take a chance of going up against Finn. It's true that, with the serum, she could kill him, but she has never administered it

18

to someone so powerful. Also, she has an ace up her sleeve, but to release that card, she would have to be desperate."

"You are making zero sense."

"There are a lot of ifs and buts when it comes to the commander. The headmistress has been looking for leverage to help her get what she wants—the Flaming Sword."

"So you've said."

"Once she realized that *you* were that leverage, she now has something that she hasn't had in a long time—hope. If she doesn't show him that she has that leverage—you—then he will be in this academy by nightfall, and there is a ninety-nine percent chance that we are all dead once he arrives."

"Good. I hope he swims in your blood."

"When did you become so bloodthirsty?"

"Somewhere between you kidnapping me and demanding two of my damn fingers! That's when."

Footsteps were approaching. Then, from around the corner, came Trev's brother, whistling a merry tune.

"Look," Trev continued, "I have a lot of explaining to do, which I promise I will, but first, I have to show my loyalty to the headmistress. If this box isn't delivered within the next twenty minutes, we are all screwed."

I held up my middle finger. "This is the only finger you are going to get."

Trev's brother laughed, causing Trev to sigh.

"Ezra, now is not the time."

The brother, Ezra, shrugged. "I could go back to my room, but I came to help."

"What?" I snapped. "Are you here to hold me down?"

Ezra leaned a solid shoulder against the empty cell in front of mine. "No. I came to take away the pain and stop the bleeding."

"Again," I said, "not getting my fingers."

"Our first priority is to stop the commander from storming the gates. Our second is to explain to you why we need you. Our third—"

"Whoa. You cannot be serious," I said. "Do you seriously think that I would *help* you?"

"Crunch, crunch, brother. We are wasting time," Ezra said.

"She feels *no* pain," Trev warned his brother.

"Of course."

I watched in horror as they took out a key and unlocked my cell. Then the limited training that I had received from the Academy of Seraph took over.

With Trev juggling the box, I kicked out a leg, catching him on his knee cap. He dropped the box, but he was able to block my escape. I grabbed a handful of his hair and pulled his face toward my rising knee. I got two good shots in before he disentangled himself from my hold. In a move that I had yet to learn, he swooped one arm under mine and had it at a weird angle within seconds. I was forced to either stop struggling or break an arm. I would have gone for the break, but logic took over. I would still have to beat Trev one-armed and, if by some miracle I whooped his ass, I would still have to go through his brother. Without my powers, there was no way I could win.

Ezra clapped. "Such a firecracker."

"Thanks for the help, brother."

Ezra shrugged. "Here, I'll help. I think she broke your nose."

"Thanks, but I already knew that."

Ezra strolled into the cell. "Listen, as highly entertaining as all this was, we are out of time." He stooped down to where the box was. Taking off the lid, he then pulled out a sharp knife. "There is good news to this. One, it will keep the headmistress from knowing your little secret. You know, the one where you're not a demi after all. And two, once your little secret is returned to you, your fingers will grow back."

I glared at him. "You need a fact-checker. I *am* a demi. The first demi to have immortality. And what is to keep either of you from telling the headmistress about my immortality?"

I couldn't see Trev's face, but Ezra looked at his brother like I was daft. "Because you are going to free us all."

I tried to turn around so I could face Trev, to plead with him not to do this, but his grip on me tightened.

"Let's get this over with," he said.

Earnestly, Ezra said, "I promise I'll heal your face, too."

"My face?" I barely had time to finish my sentence before I saw him swing his meaty fist at me. With Trev holding me tight, I could only slightly turn my head as I braced for impact. My last thought was I was going to kill them both.

five

I FELT LIKE I WAS wading through swampy water. Brown mud was all around me, and there was nothing but sloshy dirt for miles and miles. My head hurt, and my limbs felt weighted down. I was dream walking.

After searching for Finn and coming up empty, I changed tactics. I really wanted to chat with some people, but getting to them was wearing me down.

I closed my eyes as I put one foot in front of the other. I took calming breaths as I pictured the faces that I really needed to see. When I opened my eyes back up, everything around me was a pristine white, a vast difference from the slosh pit I had just waded through. My movements became easier as I almost glided on what looked like puffy, white clouds. Ahead of me was one lone door, which wasn't braced by anything, as there were no walls on either side. Tilting my chin up, I marched through the doorway.

There was a collective gasp as seven archangels noticed the intruder.

I took my time looking over all of them. Zadkiel looked more like a Viking than Ezra, with his red hair and bushy beard. One corner of his mouth climbed up as he gently tilted his head in my direction as a greeting.

Haniel stood with her mouth open. Then she bounced up and down before crossing to me, wrapping an arm around my waist. "Brothers and sister, tell me if I am imagining things, or is this really happening?"

Raphael, who had olive skin and black hair, elbowed Jeremiel, the man he was sitting next to. Jeremiel's eyes widened as he shook his dark head in disbelief. Chamuel, the one I remembered as my favorite uncle, stood slowly. Then, quicker than I could track, he was before me and had me wrapped in a bear hug. My feet left the ground as he swung me left to right. Then he peppered the top of my head with kisses.

Uriel said, "Put the poor girl down; you're going to squish her."

I smiled at him. "Hello again."

He gave me a wink, but whatever he was about to say died on his lips as my mother, who had been in the corner, let out a half-sob.

Chamuel gave her a nod. "I know. It's overwhelming. Come say hello to your daughter, Gabriel."

The woman, who looked like my older sister that was

no older than twenty-one, glided toward me. Her dark hair was tied up in a knot at the base of her neck and her beautiful blue eyes were quickly filling with unshed tears. Her ruby lips were parted as she stopped in front of me. She touched both of my cheeks before she slid her hands down my arms. When she got to my palms, she tugged them gently toward her. Tears were streaming down her face. I patted her back as she cried.

In this life, I had bounced around different foster homes and didn't have any family. Recently, I had dreams about a former life, when I had not only had a family of fifteen archangels, but they were amazing people. Or rather, angels. Their actions had caused them to fall from heaven, and only being hit with the Flaming Sword had allowed them to come back here. If, in fact, I was actually in heaven.

Because they were fallen, they had to always bear the mark of the fallen—black wings. These were all things that I had learned from dreams, but I didn't really remember the archangels. Not like how they remembered me. These people were strangers.

Sobs racked Gabriel's body as everyone else crowded around. I continued to console her awkwardly.

Finally, Uriel stepped beside Gabriel. He put an arm around her shoulders and gently pulled her back from me. After giving her a quick kiss to the temple, he said, "Let's give her a little room, shall we?"

Gabriel looked stricken for a second, like she had overstepped some sort of boundary.

I smiled at her. "You're fine. I can understand how emotional all of this must be for you."

"But you don't remember any of your first life, do you?" Chamuel asked.

Sheepishly, I said, "I'm sorry, but no."

Gabriel's spine lengthened, and for the first time, I saw the warrior inside of her. "But you will. I don't know what I have to do to return those memories, but I promise you that I will."

I didn't know what to say to that, so I gave her a nod.

Haniel grabbed my elbow and steered me to cushions that looked as soft as clouds, which reminded me of my earlier question.

After I sat down, I asked, "Am I in heaven?"

Gabriel sat to the left of me. "Yes, it's a part of heaven. We are no longer on duty, since the Flaming Sword has touched us."

Zadkiel grunted. "So much for being a *permanent* defender of earth."

"Don't be a grouchy old man," Raphael said. "We deserve vacation time."

Haniel rolled her eyes. "Let's not get started on that subject again." She sat down to my right. "Tell us, child, how was it possible for you to seek us here today?"

All seven of the archangels had found a seat and were waiting on my reply.

"I honestly don't know. My powers have been bound, and between that and the tranquilizer darts, I haven't been able to dream walk to Finn. But when I wanted to visit the seven of you to ask more questions …" I shrugged. "Well, here I am."

Jeremiel said, "Interesting. Whatever powers they have used on you only restricts you to the earth realm."

Zadkiel gave me a wink. "And you are extremely powerful. It was probably my powers that gave you such strength."

He was clearly jesting, but Jeremiel and Raphael started arguing with him.

Chamuel, ignoring them, gave me a smile. "We do peek on you often enough."

I frowned. If that was the truth, why the heck was he so cheery? Had he not seen me being kidnapped, drugged, and having my powers bound? And this was my favorite uncle?

Haniel laughed, and all of them looked at her.

She waved a hand at me. "Hello, auntie here with psychic abilities." Then she laughed again. "Her memories have told her that Chamuel was her favorite uncle."

Chamuel beamed while the other four men in the room all started arguing and denying that statement.

I sighed. She had picked up my thoughts, and that was what had concerned her?

She grabbed my hand. "Sweetheart, Azrael gave you an amazing gift. As long as you don't burn through your powers without recuperating, you can't be killed. And this so-called binding that they wrapped around your brain"—

she gently touched my forehead-"is only lasting because you haven't fought against it. Once your powers come back to you, if you choose to, you could bring the Empowered Academy down with everyone in it."

Gabriel piped up, "Though we don't recommend that. In fact, we think you shouldn't fight against the binding."

"Um ... why?" I asked.

It was Raphael who said, "We believe that everything happens for a very good reason. You are at that academy for a reason."

Haniel butted in, "One that I will not disclose, but I can say that you will be helping innocents if you just let destiny carry you for a moment."

Jeremiel nodded. "You're heading for big things."

That all sounded fine and great, but there was one thing that I was very unhappy with.

"Right before I was kidnapped, I had a dream about the day that all of you were touched by the Flaming Sword ... the day of my wedding."

There was sorrow in their gazes.

"I learned that I was to marry Finn in my previous life. There is a torrent of emotions going on inside of me, and I would really like to talk with him, but with this binding around my mind—" I rubbed a hand over my chest—"I can no longer seek him or feel him."

Gabriel nodded. "I can understand how that would make you feel. Please understand that Finn is on his own path. It's very different from yours, but just as much needed by the blessed. You are their champion, but so is he."

"And you will get to talk with him again soon," Haniel added.

I silently wondered how good of a psychic she was.

She laughed, her long, pale neck tilted back as she held her belly. Finally, she said, "I'm the best. I assure you that you will see your Finn again, and soon. Patience, my dear."

Chamuel said, "Besides, the binding Finn did recently is a better memory than your wedding would have been."

If I hadn't been paying attention, I wouldn't have noticed Gabriel and Haniel subtly shaking their heads, or Uriel wincing.

"What's going on?" I asked.

Chamuel took a look at his brothers and sisters and said, "Hmm? What's that?"

I narrowed my eyes. "Would you still like to be the favorite uncle or not?"

Uriel laughed. "You know, little one, some things aren't for us to tell."

I crossed my arms over my chest. "I don't mean to be disrespectful, but considering that I have a whole life that I can no longer remember, maybe you could throw some much-needed info my way."

Gabriel squeezed my hand. "I plan on getting my daughter's memories back, and Haniel can give you as much as you need to know without altering your path, but as far as the binding that Finn put on you, that is between the two of you. Now, do you have any other questions that you think Haniel might be able to answer?"

Thinking, I gnawed my bottom lip. "How about the six that I'm supposed to choose? Can you help me know who, when, and how I'm to transfer some of the power of the Flaming Sword to them?"

Jeremiel said, "You have the power of eight archangels inside of you and—"

"Eight, for sure?" I interrupted. "I mean, we knew from my dreams that I had seven, and then we thought there was a chance that Haniel had given me some of her power, but I wasn't certain."

Jeremiel nodded. "Yes, unfortunately, since you came into your powers, you really haven't had the opportunity to learn, to let your powers manifest organically. Everything has been such a whirlwind, but once the binding is removed from your mind, you will be flooded with power."

That sounded intense.

Haniel grabbed my other hand and rubbed in gently. "You will be fine."

"Once the binding is removed," Jeremiel said, "and you're in control of your powers again, remember to truly embrace them."

Chamuel nodded. "My gift will help you. When you go to make a difficult decision, let your gut lead you. If you truly rely on it, then you will either feel confident in your decision or almost violently ill." He gave me a charming wink. "Literally, follow your gut."

Haniel's eyes glazed over for a bit before she smiled at

me. "You have a visitor waiting for you to wake up."

"Finn?" I asked.

"Afraid not."

Gabriel's face contorted with sadness. "Oh, but she can't go. I've waited so long for this … for when we are finally back together." She looked around at her brothers and sister. "She can't just go right now."

"Sister," Haniel started, "we can't keep her here. She has her own journey to live. She is part of the prophecy."

Uriel nodded. "Think of *why* we need her."

"*Everyone* needs her." Gabriel's words had a bite to them.

"This is true," Chamuel stated. "A lot of people depend on her. We can't let our own selfishness get in the way."

Gabriel threw her dainty hands up in frustration. "I wasn't saying forever. I just thought we would have a little more time together on our reunion day."

My heart hurt for her. I might not remember her, but that was a one-way street. The way she looked at me was like I was still her little girl.

I wrapped my arms around her and gave her a long hug, this time without the awkward patting. When I released her, she wiped her tears, and my uncles gave me nods and thumbs-up.

Knowing what she needed to hear, I said, "Mom, I promise that these visits aren't over. I'll be able to find you again."

Just by me labeling her as a parent made her mouth drop open before she gave me a radiant smile. Then she enveloped my face in her hands and kissed both my cheeks. "I will hold you to that."

I stood up and smiled at the archangels.

Chamuel gave me a sheepish look. "And if you could wait for your gut to tell you it's time to shed the binding around your mind, I would—we would all—be forever grateful."

"Can I at least ask why?"

He nodded. "We don't want the headmistress of the academy to know what she has allowed behind her doors until it's too late."

"Let the one who bound you take it off." Haniel gave me a nod of encouragement. "It will hurt less than you breaking through the barrier that he put around your mind." She gave me a wink. "You better hurry. Your visitor grows impatient."

With a push, I fell through the whiteness then back through the mud at a much faster rate than it had taken me initially.

My heart felt warm as I shook off the dredges of sleep.

SIX

"OH LAWD, CHILD. YOU LOOK like the first time I met you—a hella mess."

The visit with the archangels still fresh in my mind, I opened my eyes and looked around in confusion. I saw Remy standing there, looking like a ray of freaking sunshine. She was in my cell.

No, this had to be another dream.

"Remy?" I squeaked out.

"In the flesh, baby. And I do mean, in the flesh." She sat down on the nasty floor, her nose wrinkling in disgust as she did so. Her black hair with the tips dyed red swayed as she took in my surroundings. Remy was one of my two best friends and having her here had me smiling from ear to ear.

"Well," she said, "this is uber depressing."

I threw my arms around her. "I know it's only been a

couple of days, but man, I missed you."

She patted my back. "Yeah, I've missed you, too."

"So, how did you know I was here?"

"I followed you in ghost form. I'd like to add that I'm really getting a handle on becoming corporal when I need to be. I'm not rating myself, but if I were that narcissistic, I'd be an eleven out of ten."

I felt the beginnings of the first genuine smile since all of this had happened.

"As soon as I saw your exact location, I reported back to Finn." She winced. "The poor dude is going crazy. He didn't feel your bond, and I thought he was going to destroy the whole world."

My heart clenched. "Yeah, Trev's brother, Ezra, did something to me." I tapped my temple. "I'm not sure what the exact terminology is, but it has bound my powers, and I can no longer feel Finn."

She narrowed her blue eyes with rage. "I could kill Trev and this stupid brother of his."

"I might not have my powers currently, but when I did have them, I never felt like Trev wanted to cause me harm."

"Yeah, well, I guess you're not perfect after all, because that was a huge mistake on your part."

"Or maybe he doesn't really wish me harm." I grabbed her arm. "I'm assuming that Finn is on his way?"

"Duh. Like the big, bad wolf, he's going to be singing for these little piggies to let him in. He plans on bringing this academy down, brick by brick. I just have to get you out of here first. Talk to Mama. You haven't seen a key, by any chance, have you?"

I shook my head. "Sorry. They didn't conveniently tell me where the key to my escape would be between darting me with that damn tranquilizer gun and me getting accustomed to my new quarters."

"Smartass," Remy said. "Everyone is a smartass." She disappeared in front of my eyes. Then I heard her from the other side of the bars. "I should leave your perky butt behind. It would serve you right for being snarky with the queen."

"If your high-ass could hurry along; we don't have much time, and I personally would like to be out of this building before Finn starts tearing it apart."

"Oh, the demands," she quipped.

"Also, I need to tell you that I just dream walked to the seven archangels who had fallen under the blade of the Flaming Sword. They believe that I'm on the correct path that I need to be."

I heard her grab something. "Seriously? They were right here? What freaking amateurs."

I rolled my eyes. She clearly wasn't listening, but I would bet anything she would be mad at me later for not sharing.

She came back toward me in the flesh, dangling the keys. "Don't give me that look. I heard you. So, if I'm here with your freedom, then this is a part of your destiny. We don't really have time for tea leaves and journal entries, so we need to go if we're going."

I smiled at my friend. She was a nut. A nut who was rescuing me.

As she put the key in the lock, I bounced from foot to foot with nervous energy. I didn't release my breath until the door to my freedom swung open. Then I threw my arms around Remy.

"Girl, all of these hugs have got me feeling some sort of way. I have told you that I'm straight, right? I mean, you're cute and all, but you just don't do it for me."

I pulled back from her, and she caught sight of my bandaged hand, stained with blood. "What the hell happened?"

"Trev and his maniac brother took two of my fingers; that's what happened."

"You're kidding me?"

I waved the bandaged hand in her face. "Would I lie about something crazy like that? Miraculously, it doesn't hurt. At all, actually. Also, they said they were delivering my appendages to Finn so that he wouldn't storm the academy and kill everyone."

Remy was so mad that her jaw was clenched. "You think the commander is mad now? Wait until I deliver you to him, and he sees what they have done to you."

I nodded. Getting back to Finn sounded great to me. The archangels said I would see him soon. I guessed I was just afraid to hope that it would be today.

"Okay, what is the plan now?"

She pursed her lips. "I just have to get you outside.

35

Once we are outdoors, the commander said he would take care of the rest. Obviously, we can't leave the way I came, because you're not a hot ghost. Plus, there's a small problem. We didn't know that someone had bound your powers. I mean, this brother of jerk-face would have to know how powerful you are, and it's not like you would go around broadcasting that."

I didn't say anything as she tapped a finger to her lips. The archangels made it clear that they didn't want me to shed the binding around my mind, but if I told Remy that, she would have a conniption fit.

"Okay, this is what we are going to do. There are three levels of cells. These people are sadistic, by the way. You are the only one on this level, but the other two levels above us are jam-packed, which makes me wonder why—"

I snapped my fingers in front of her face. "Concentrate. Escape."

"Okay, okay. So, we go up two levels, and then we look for a side door. It's almost dark, so we find a side exit and make a run for it. I'll be in ghost form, so anyone who comes at you, I'll slow them down."

"And what am I supposed to do? Just leave you?"

"Dude, I'm literally a ghost—can't die."

"Good point."

"You ready?"

I nodded. "I was ready the moment you came into my cell. Let's go."

I watched as my friend disappeared again. Without my

powers, I couldn't see her when she was in ghost form. Damn Trev and his stupid brother.

An Arctic wind blasted me, causing me to shiver.

"Easy, dude. You just ran straight through me," she chided.

"Hello! No powers. Therefore, you are invisible to me. We should be grateful that I can still hear you."

"I hate Trev and his brother."

"Me, too. He is at the top of my hate list."

"Cute. You have a list. Stick to the right side of the stairwell. I'll be on the left. And no more talking."

I followed behind her quietly, thinking about what the archangels had said. Haniel had commented that, if I let Trev's brother take the binding off, it would hurt less. She was psychic. Was she giving me a suggestion or advice? If I escaped with Remy, would I even see Trev or his brother again?

We went up a flight of steps, but before we could continue, we heard someone coming. I went through the open door that would take us to the holding cells right above, where I was hoping Remy followed. When I felt a brush of cold air, I relaxed a little. I was in trouble, but having her there made the weight sitting on my shoulders a little easier to bear.

I pointed to what looked like another door at the end of the corridor, but then a whimper froze me in my tracks, and I looked to the right.

Two girls, under the age of ten but looked identical,

were huddled together on the cold floor. I knew I looked dirty, but these girls were downright filthy. Their hair might have been blonde, but it was too hard to tell, as the matted mess hung around their shoulders. There were purple marks under their big, brown eyes.

"I can't leave them."

Remy hissed, "We will come back for them. It's risky enough with just you. How are we going to escape with two children? No, no, and no."

"Damn it, Remy! Give me the keys."

She materialized before me and handed me the pair of keys, all while shaking her head. "This is crazy. I can clearly see your freedom slipping away."

I opened the door, yet the girls remained huddled on the ground, staring at Remy.

I gave them a small smile. "My friend has some pretty cool tricks. If you want to stay here, then I won't force you, but if you want to be free, you need to get up right now, be quiet, and follow me."

The twins both nodded as they stood, still clinging to one another. The only difference between them was one girl's eyes were a lighter shade of brown. She was the one who reached for my hand. I gave her fingers a reassuring squeeze before we started walking again.

Others started calling out from the darkened cells. Pleas washed over me as I stood there, gripping a little girl's hand. How many more of these people were children? From one of the cells, farther down, I heard a baby crying.

Rage boiled in the pit of my stomach.

An old man, who was stooped so far over it looked like he was reaching for his toes, leaned up against the bars. "Lassie, you can't take them with you. They are marked. They won't make it past the lavender fields."

Before I could ask what the heck that meant, I heard a noise that immediately quieted all the pleas.

Remy said, "Well, shit," just as the sound of boots came toward us. There was no way we would make it to the door in time.

Trev came around the corner with a tray full of food. His eyes landed on me, then Remy, then the little girls.

The one child jerked out of my grip. Then both girls ran to him, throwing their arms around his lower body.

He balanced the tray with one hand as he gave each girl a half-hug and whispered, "I'm sorry. The headmistress wouldn't let me come see you both until I brought back the girl you were just standing with." He rubbed their backs while they cried. "The headmistress just cleared both of your releases today. Everything is going to be okay."

One of the girls wiped the snot from her nose then pointed at me. "Is she an angel?"

He smiled back. "I think so, yes."

The other child said, "Are we really free?"

He nodded, clearly not able to reply. There was so much emotion swirling in his eyes. Then he took a step to the right, almost dragging one child with him as he set the tray on a small table that was between cells.

"Girls, eat this food. Then I'll take you to get baths, and we'll spend some time together, catching up."

The girl who had held my hand trembled. "Brother, I was so scared."

"I know, Ana." His hand shook as he wiped away a tear from her small face.

Remy took a step back. "Well, this has been a high-grade, Hallmark-quality bull"—she looked at the little girls—"crap, but I feel like I've seen this episode, and I don't care for the rerun, so we're going to bounce."

Would Trev just let me walk out of here?

He gave me a nod before he watched the girls tear into the food. "Easy, girls. Go slow." He then walked toward me, and I tensed.

"You have no reason to trust me—none. I want to say one thing, though, then you can make your decision. If you still want to leave, then I'll help create a distraction."

"Oh please," Remy drawled. "Where's the mute button?"

Ignoring her, he continued, "Do you see my sisters? They have never done anything to anyone, and yet the headmistress went to our home and took them from my mother. Do you know why?"

Remy rolled her eyes. "Dude, we ain't got time for your drama." She grabbed my arm and started to pull me toward the door.

Trev sighed. "That door leads to a utility closet. You'll have to go back the way you came."

Remy saluted him as she started tugging me back toward

the door that we had initially slipped in from.

As we passed him, he said, "The headmistress took them because she needed incentive for me to go to the Academy of Seraph. She knew there was a good chance that the commander would kill me on sight. She also wanted to remind me of what she held in these cells. That way, I would work harder on finding Finn's weakness."

"Me."

He nodded. "You."

Remy stomped her foot. "Oh em gee, people. Now is not the time." She pointed a finger at Trev. "You suck. You want her to know why you suck. Okay, we heard you. Can we go now?"

He furrowed his eyebrows. "Do I know you?"

"Ugh. No, but I know you, and I have to tell you ... I am super unimpressed."

Trev turned his attention back to me. "There are people here who don't want to be here, but they are forced to, because someone they love is being held in these cells. Just like they were forced to be called darken, but they should have an opportunity to shed that name. They should have an opportunity to be called blessed. They should have an opportunity to choose and be free." He hit a switch on the wall, and light bulbs flickered on, showing the inside of the darkened cells. People of all different ages, including a mother with a newborn baby, were in the cells. They blinked as they tried to adjust to the onslaught of light.

"Why are you showing me this?"

"The commander is powerful, but he will not be able to free these people. When he barges in here, halfcocked and crazed, what will he accomplish? He will be walking in on a situation that he knows nothing about. These people"— he nodded toward the people who had started to cling to the bars that separated us—"will be caught in the crossfire, and I can promise you it won't stop there. The hell that the headmistress will release upon earth can destroy mankind. The only person who can free these people is you."

"How?"

"Tell me you're not buying this bullcrap?" Remy asked. "Dude, he literally took your fingers."

She pointed again at Trev. "Our boy Finn is going to kill you. Dead is what you are."

"How?" I asked again, a little more forcible.

He took several steps closer to me, making Remy move in closer, too. We looked like we were about to have a powwow before a soccer game.

Trev whispered, "That thing you have that can kill even the most powerful—"

"For shit's sake, man"—Remy narrowed her eyes—"tell me he doesn't know about *the thing*."

I bit my lip and nodded. "I didn't tell him, though. Remember, he just witnessed it when I was dealing with Zack." I had actually killed the boy, but I wasn't at a point in my life where I could own that just yet. "And this might be a good time to tell you his brother knows, as well, about *the thing*."

"You have got to be freaking kidding me," Remy said. "Why don't we just mark an *X* on your back or send out postcards in the mail, announcing what you can do? Maybe you could give out coupons and discounts during the holidays. Anyone who wants to take a selfie with the demi who carries the you-know-what gets fifteen percent off portraits today only."

"Why have something if you don't use it?" Trev asked, ignoring her. "I get why the commander wants to keep your secret, but if you play it safe, what is the point of having this power? Think of the people you can save."

Uriel's words, along with the other archangels, came to me as I took in the prisoners around me. Yes, I could escape, but could I live with myself? These people needed me.

I tilted my head toward the stooped-over old man who was still looking at us like ninety percent of the other prisoners. "He said something about how I wouldn't get too far with the girls because they were marked. What did he mean?"

"We all carry a mark that resembles a feather somewhere on us. It keeps us bound to the academy unless the headmistress has given us special permission to leave the grounds. If you don't have permission and you try to leave or escape, you will be hit with a pain that feels like your bones are melting. If you are mortal ... like most of these people, you will die from the pain."

I looked over his shoulder at his sisters. I could have hurt them, killed them by trying to take them from this place,

43

and I didn't even know.

He saw the look that crossed my face. "Don't worry; I would have gotten to them before too much damage happened, and Ezra would have healed them. You were just trying to help."

Remy rolled her eyes so many times that I thought they would bounce out of her head. "Oh, good play, lover boy, good play."

"You are literally our Trojan horse," Trev continued, still ignoring Remy. "You are the answer to our prayers."

A small boy coughed from one of the cells to my left. His mom wiped his tawny brown hair from his brow. Then she jerked her gaze to meet mine. There was a silent plea in them. She didn't know who I was, and she didn't care. If Trev was putting his faith in me, then so was she. There was no masking the hope in her eyes.

"All of these people are being used by the headmistress?"

"Yes, and if their loved one dies while trying to complete a mission, then they will remain in these cells until their dying day." He pointed to the mother and child who I had just observed. "Kass and her son have been in here since he was two. He is now five."

I clenched my fists at my sides. How could a mother raise a child in an eight-by-ten cell? Did he even remember what it felt like to be out in the sun? Or chase other children? My heart wanted to see Finn, but that was not what it needed. It *needed* to help these people.

My exchange with Uriel came floating back to me. If I

walked out of here right now and chose safety, I knew I wouldn't be able to live with myself. These people needed me.

Remy saw where my train of thought was going and pointed a finger into Trev's chest. "I don't like you. I just wanted to get that out of the way."

Trev bit back a smile. "Duly noted."

Looking at me, he said, "I am a prisoner here. Those men, women, and children are captives too. I'm sorry that I was forced to hurt you. I'm sorry about a lot of things. I need you to stay so we can take down the key players together. Free these people. I can't do it by myself. Do we have a deal?"

I took one more look at the little boy on my left. "Yeah, we have a deal. But if you cross me again, I can promise you that it will be your last day on earth."

Trev nodded. Then he gave all his attention to Remy. "How did you get in here without setting off any of the school's wards or alerting the guards?"

She narrowed her blue eyes. "I have my ways."

"Well, whatever they are, I'm going to need you to carry a message to the commander." He started walking toward the door. "Let's get Gabriella back to her cell before the guards do their walkthrough."

Grabbing each of his sisters by the hand, he pulled them toward the door. Then he knelt before them. "Ezra is showing your discharge papers to the guard above. He is waiting for you both on the next level. I want you both to walk up the stairs and go with him. In half an hour, the four of us will eat ice cream and celebrate. Okay?"

They both nodded and gave their older brother a quick hug before dashing up the stairs. He stood still for a moment, just breathing deeply as he tried to get his emotions under control. Once he did, he turned toward us.

I was mad at Trev, but my heart understood why he had done what he did. If I would have been in his shoes I would have done the same thing. Trev was a good person that was faced with hard decisions. After taking one look at his sister's tiny faces that were filled with hope I knew that he made the right decision.

We walked back the way we had come, taking the flight of steps down to the lowest part of the building. Remy was uncharacteristically quiet. She gnawed her lip as she was lost in her thoughts. Trev looked like he carried the weight of the world on his shoulders. After witnessing all those desperate faces, I could honestly see why he felt that way.

Remy said, "This is so stupid. I'll be shocked if the commander doesn't kick my scrawny butt. You see one kid with big doe eyes, and your escape was nothing but a pipedream. And what if we are being tricked?"

Trev turned toward her. "I swear on everything that I love that this is not a trick. We need her. Our people need to be freed, and she is the key to their freedom."

Trev paced the dirty corridor before he turned to both of us. "I think I know what you are capable of, Gabriella, and if I'm right, then that little boy, along with his mother,

Kass, could be freed by tomorrow. He could be chasing fireflies after supper." He stopped walking and came to stand before me. "I know you hate me now"—he gave me a boyish smile—"and any hope I had of making you fall in love with me is probably gone, but in order for this to work, I'm going to need you to trust me."

"Trev," I said at the same time that Remy started laughing.

I narrowed my eyes at her, and she threw up her hands.

"Girl, I get it. You're a good person. You decided to stay and help strangers. I personally don't have that affliction, but then again, I'm not winning any humanitarian awards. But just keep in mind the guy who lied to you—"

"I actually did tell her that I would do anything for my sisters. I also told her not to trust anybody," Trev interrupted.

"Yep." Remy looked at me. "And how many times were you darted, girlfriend?"

I shrugged. "I lost count."

She laughed without mirth. "She lost count. That's how many. Then you took her fingers. Look, she is going to help you, and I will be helping her, but ain't nobody here has to trust you. Trust is earned, not given."

Remy looked two seconds away from hitting Trev, so I cleared my throat as I walked back into my cell. I prayed I wasn't making the biggest mistake of my life.

He was shutting the door and locking it when we heard footsteps.

Trev's eyes widened in fear as he grabbed Remy by the arm and started pulling her toward a janitorial closet, but whoever was coming our way was coming fast, and they would never make it to the closet.

He stopped mid-stride when her wrist disappeared from his grasp. The look on his face was ludicrous at best. He was still trying to process what had happened when Ezra approached, his hazel eyes narrowed as he took in the panicked look on Trev's face.

"What the hell is wrong with you, brother?"

Trev stood up straight. "Nothing. I thought I saw a ghost." He laughed as he ran a hand down the back of his neck. "Why are you down here? And where are the girls?"

Ezra was still staring at his brother strangely. "Luna took the girls to get baths. They smell horrible. She said they would meet us in your room in thirty. Give us time to plan." He tilted his head in my direction. "I came to ask you if the box made it to the commander yet."

Trev nodded. "I'd think so by now. If not, any minute now."

I looked at the space I had last seen Remy. Finn was going to go ballistic. I needed her to get to him before that box arrived.

Ezra took one more look at me before he sighed and walked back down the corridor to the exit. He was mumbling something about us all dying before he completely disappeared from our view.

Within seconds, Remy reappeared.

"I don't believe it. How could this be?" Trev asked.

"I'll catch you up to speed later," I promised.

His brown eyes met mine. "Is this your doing?"

I refused to answer.

"Wow. You are way more powerful than I ever believed. Amazing."

Remy snapped her fingers in front of his face. "What do you want me to relay back to the commander? I need to get to him before princess's fingers arrive."

"Yes, of course. Tell him what you saw here today in the cells. Tell him, if he will be patient and help us win this battle, I will help him with the war that is yet to come. Tell him that Gabriella has willingly agreed to help. I'm meeting with my friends now. We will come up with a plan then tell him what to do."

Remy rolled her eyes. "Yeah, the commander doesn't really like to be told what to do."

"Remy," I said, "just give him the message." I cut my eyes to Trev. "Also, tell him my powers have been bound. It also did something to our bond, but reassure him that I'm fine. And tell him that, if my fingers don't return when my powers do, he can personally kill Trev while we all watch."

"Why exactly were her powers bound?" Remy asked.

"My brother did it at my request," Trev said. "We had to. The headmistress has a powerful ally who can sense powers. If she knew how truly powerful Gabriella is, we would all be in trouble. We need Gabriella to be just an object that the commander wants, not an object that could kill the headmistress."

To think, not so long ago, I didn't want to be blessed, didn't want powers, didn't want to be a part of this world, and now I was aggravated that my powers were bound.

Remy grabbed ahold of the front of Trev's shirt. "But you are positive that it can be undone? She will get her powers back?"

"Of course," Trev said. "But, my brother is the only one who can undo it."

"Or, if your brother dies," Remy said, "I'm assuming that would lift the bind he put on her."

"Well, yes. But I'd prefer my brother not die in order to lift the binding."

"Regardless," Remy said as she let him go, "I'll tell the commander. That way, he can keep his options open."

I tried hard not to laugh. My bestie was a savage. I needed to tell her that, according to the archangels, I could lift the binding at any time, but I didn't want to say that in front of Trev.

Remy gave my good hand that was holding the bar a squeeze. "I'll deliver this message, and then I'll come back and keep you company."

I should tell her no, but the truth was that I really didn't want to be by myself. "Thank you."

She disappeared, leaving Trev and me alone.

Trev turned the lock to my cell. "You will be saving a lot of innocent lives. Never forget that, okay?"

Well, that sounded omniscient.

"Go work out a plan so I can get out of this hellhole."

He gave me a smile before he left the same way his brother had.

I went back to my corner and crouched down on the dirty floor. I either just made the best decision of my life or the stupidest. Either way, I knew that Finn was going to be livid.

seven

I WAS PACING THE SMALL confines of my cell when I heard someone popping their bubble gum. I turned to see Remy rubbing dust off her fingers. Something was off about her body language. It was like she was trying to act chill.

"You're back already?"

"Yeah."

"That's it? Just *yeah*? What did Finn say?"

She sighed. "Truth?"

I nodded.

"When I say it didn't go too well, I mean it as an understatement. Your boy ran his fist through a tree. Like, an actual hickory tree. The scariest part is he didn't even flinch. I almost passed out just from seeing the broken bones in his hand. But then, when I had the nerve to actually look at his face, I think I peed a little. Being a ghost, I no longer have that function, ya know, so part of me is like, 'Whoop, whoop. Bodily functions again, yay,' and then the other part of me is like, 'Can I die again?'"

"Did you tell him why I did what I did?"

"Yeah, but dude, he can't care about all these people when all he can think about is you." She sat next to me. "It took him a minute to get himself under control, but he's better now."

I nodded. To have waited all this time for me to come back, just to feel like he lost me again … I could only imagine what he was going through.

"So, you made it before the box?"

"Yeah." Her eyes widened. "Oh crap, I forgot to tell him that the box with a couple of your fingers was coming and to be prepared."

"Are you freaking kidding me?"

She pointed a finger at me. "Don't yell at me. I panicked. The commander is scary AF. Plus, Hannah was there, and you know how she is."

"How is Hannah?"

Remy rolled her eyes. "The girl hasn't stopped crying. It's like a faucet that no one can turn off. I told her you were fine, and she screeched in my ear, '*Fine? Fine?*' and then she started crying louder. You know who else isn't fine?"

"Who?"

Her lips curled into a smile. "Dan and Richard. I think they grew really attached to you. They have done nothing but mope around since you left. It's almost comical." She bit her lip. "They will also flip when they see the box. I guess I need to go back and calm them down."

I pictured the two meatheads in my mind. I called them "The Rocks" because they looked like Dwayne Johnson. To think of them pouting was hilarious.

"You think we made the right choice?" I asked.

She shrugged. "Before coming here, I went to the cells above you and looked around. You know that mom you saw?"

I nodded.

"She was pacing the small confines of that room while her son slept in a corner full of dirt and spiderwebs. That is no way to raise a child. They deserve better. I still don't trust Trev, but if you're the key to that child getting an actual room with a bed, then I say let's do this. Together."

I grabbed her hand and squeezed. "Thank you."

"I just wanted to clarify something really quick," she said. "Who do you love more—Hannah or me? I mean, say we were on a stranded island, and you could only save one, who would you pick? The girl who is awesome in every sense of the word or the freakishly large giraffe who could float an island with her waterworks?"

I laughed. "Oh, I didn't know it was a competition. I can't say both?"

"What kind of loser says both?"

I tapped a finger to my chin. "Well, Hannah doesn't name call."

"But she's also not in a stinky cell with you either."

"Yeah," I said, "but she has been crying nonstop over me."

"Dude. Like, so much. It's beyond ridic. Honestly, I'm in here with you not because I love you but just to escape her."

I was laughing until she shushed me. "Someone is coming."

"Disappear," I said. "Right now, you are my secret weapon."

She was gone before Trev rounded the corner with the headmistress.

She was petite and slim, with raven hair that fell to her bottom and swayed with every step she took toward my cell. She had a five-finger forehead, wide-set eyes, and thin lips. The only thing really going for her was her high cheekbones. Her black dress was so sheer I could almost see through it. Overall, she was average-looking, but the way she carried herself made one want to stop and take notice. Power. She reeked of power.

I didn't say a word as she stopped right in front of my cell. I shifted my eyes to Trev, who was trying to convey some sort of message with his own eyes, one I wasn't getting.

"It has been three days since you have been brought here, and we have not received word from the commander, even though our sources say that he has received the box. He should be here by now." Her voice was loud and precise. "What is your relationship with the commander of the Academy of Seraph?"

There was a slight shake of Trev's head.

Going with my gut, I said, "I don't have one with the commander."

"You obviously do, or Trev wouldn't have reported back to me that you were the answer to weakening the commander," she said.

"Headmistress," Trev cut in, "if I may?"

She studied him for a brief moment then nodded.

"When I reported to you that the commander was infatuated with this girl, I didn't realize that it was completely one-sided." He cleared his throat. "This could work out even better than I imagined."

Her nose flared. "What are you proposing? And know that, if you fail me, I will put your sisters back in their proper place. I'm sure they miss their cell."

Just because I was closely watching, I noticed Trev clench his fists then release.

"I won't fail you. Look at her."

The headmistress took all of me in.

"She can be an asset. Let her lure him in. Not just for information on the Flaming Sword, but what if he was on our side against any who tried to take the sword from you once you obtain it?"

"Do you think I'm stupid?" the headmistress snarled, her ruby red lips curled back from pearly white teeth. "How did you think I was going to be able to command the commander? Once he is turned, I will know exactly where the Flaming Sword is. He will have no way of disobeying me. But I need him here in order to do that."

I looked at Trev. His face had registered shock then panic.

Turned? Turned to what? A darken? There was no way Finn would be swayed to her side. I didn't know what was going through Trev's mind, but he wasn't really selling this to the headmistress. She wanted an immediate plan of action, or heads were going to roll.

I cleared my throat. "Excuse me, um … Headmistress?"

Her eyes flashed to mine.

"You are making very valid points, but I'd like to say that I'm not just a girl."

Trev was slightly shaking his head, and I could feel cold air pressing up against me—Remy's way of telling me to shut up.

"The commander actually believes that I'm his soulmate."

For a second, no one moved. Even the cold air that had been swirling around me froze at my words.

"Why wouldn't you tell me this, Trevan?" Her voice grew louder with each word.

I answered for him. "He didn't know. That's not something the commander would broadcast because that makes me his Achille's heel. Here's the thing; I don't think that he is my soulmate. It's no secret that I didn't want to be a part of any of this, and I'm sure your spies could tell you that I was very unhappy at the academy. I'm sure that you are also aware that I was forced to the academy after years of avoiding anything that was angel blessed. I will willingly get the information you seek if you promise to let me go after all of this. I don't want to be a part of your world."

The headmistress gave me a calculating look. "Silly girl, you are nothing but a lure. That is where your only worth lies."

I tilted my head. "Well, then let me be a lure. Hopefully, after all this, you will let me join you here at the Empowered Academy?"

She tapped a long-painted nail on her lower lip. "You want to be a darken?"

Looking her into the eyes, I said, "Anything that goes against what the commander is for, I'm all in."

She turned to Trev. "Take her out of this cell, clean her up, and then bring her to the party tonight. If she passes Thalan's test, then I will believe her and she will live. Then I will formulate an appropriate plan that will allow me to use her to the best of her abilities."

She meant as bait.

Trev gave her a curt nod.

Her eyes flashed to me. "Don't disappoint me, little one, or I'll drain you slowly."

I had to force my eyes down to seem less disobedient.

I waited until the sound of her heels went from faint to nonexistent before I lifted my gaze to Trev. He was fuming mad.

Remy appeared by my side, equally livid.

I threw my hands up in surrender. "What did you guys want me to do?"

"Um, not that," Remy said.

Trev said, "I don't like the huge target you just put on yourself. Soulmates are rare, and that word can't be thrown around."

Before Remy could jump in, as well, I held up a hand to stop her. "The headmistress could have come down here to torture me for information, or she could have thought I was a waste of time and tried to have me killed."

Trev furrowed his brows. "Once you have your powers back, can you even be killed?"

I shrugged. Again, not wanting to tell Trev what Haniel had said about the only way I could die was if I exhausted my powers and still tried to continue to use them, I said, "I really don't know, but I can honestly say I don't want to test the theory out."

"If Gabriella can't be killed, then there would be a lot of questions." Trev smiled.

"Who is Thalan?" I asked.

"He is the headmistress's right-hand man. He is a fallen angel who has conquered the art of dark magic. He is extremely powerful, like Sariel, from the Academy of Seraph. But he doesn't need to consult the cards. He will know how powerful you are by just being near you."

"That's why you had my powers bound?"

"Yes," he said. "If anyone here knows who you really are, then it's game over." He pointed at my bandage. "Hiding who you are until we're ready is imperative. Let's hope that my brother is as good as I think he is."

Remy fake-yawned. "Wow, this convo has been super

enlightening, but here is what I'm going to need from you, betrayer of friends." She waved an arm around my cell. "This isn't The Ritz-Carlton. Can we get her released, like, now? And what is the plan for freeing these people?"

He grabbed the key and released me from the cell. "I'm working on the finer details. You are just going to have to—"

"Trust you?" I said, making him wince. "I have people outside of this wall who care about me. People who are confused as to why I would willingly stay in a prison. Whatever your plan is needs to be acted out immediately. I don't want this to drag out. I want to help these people, but I also want out of this academy. Do you understand?"

"More than you will ever realize." His eyes met mine, and they were filled with regret and something more.

"Trev …"

He shook his head. "No, I know. I found the box, you know."

What? "The box with my fingers?"

"No, the commander has that." He looked at Remy. "You told him, right?"

"I accidentally forgot"—she winced—"but I'm going now."

He held up a hand. "I think Gabriella is going to need you for the next couple hours."

I waved my hands back and forth. "Hello, what box are we talking about?" Then it hit me, and I found myself angry all over again. "You took his memory box that day at his cabin?"

"Yeah, and when I looked inside, that's when I knew. I saw items that belonged to you—the ring, the lock of hair, the love letters. I had heard stories of the love that the commander had lost, but no one knew that the girl would be coming back centuries later. I'm happy for him." He shuffled his feet. "I'm happy for you."

Remy ping-ponged back and forth between us before she held an arm above her head. "Look, I don't really like you, but if you're looking for a quick rebound, I hear that angry—"

"Remy!" I interrupted. "Don't finish that sentence."

Trev laughed as Remy tried to act all innocent. "Whaaat? I'm just saying, if he wanted to use me for extracurricular purposes, then I guess I could do him a solid, even though that hot brother of his is more my speed. He has got this feral look to him that is calling me to tame the inner beast."

I rubbed my temples as I started to feel the beginnings of a migraine coming on.

Trev tracked my motions with a frown. "We need to act quickly. I think Gabriella's body is trying to shed the binding my brother put on her."

"My head is killing me."

Remy bit her lip. "We need to get to this party and pass whatever test the headmistress will have her run through, and then you"—she pointed a finger at Trev's defined chest—"better have a worthy plan. You don't want to make me angry ... er."

Trev grabbed my elbow. "Let's get you upstairs and cleaned up. I'll put out some feelers to see what it is we need to expect tonight."

Once again, Remy disappeared, though I felt her beside me as we left the lowest level. The cold air was never getting too far from me.

Trev's face changed as we entered what seemed to be the first ground level of the building. Students congregated around the lobby. Some were reclining on couches, and some stood by, holding up the walls. Trev wore a stoic mask on his face as he ushered me up a spiral staircase.

I could feel the students of the Empowered's eyes on me. I lifted my chin and met everyone's eyes that lingered too long in my direction. I gave them my best I'm-here-whatcha-going-to-do-about-it? look. Finally, after three flights of steps, Trev ushered me into a room.

"Hopefully, if tonight goes well, there will be no more cells in your future. For now, though, I'm going to put you in this room. It is right beside my sisters. Mine and my brother's are right across the hall. The room on the other side of you belongs to my best friend, Luna. So, basically, you are surrounded by people who will be loyal to you." He pointed to a gown on the bed. "Anticipating your release, I asked my brother for a favor. The dress probably won't fit, but Ezra borrowed it for you from one of his lady friends."

Remy popped up beside me. "Wait—what? My future hubby is a slut? Oh no, this isn't going to go good for him." She went over to the bed and fingered the side of the dress like it was about to attack her. "Who wore this? Will my best friend, the one I would donate a kidney for, die or contract a nasty disease from putting this garment on her porcelain oh-my-gosh-I-need-some-sun-because-I've-been-in-a-dungeon body?"

Trev stared at her for a minute like he was flabbergasted and couldn't come up with anything to say. Finally, he shook his head. "So, I'm going to head out so I can come up with a plan on how to recuse the ones below. I need to inquire how to get the mark off of them without anyone knowing that I'm asking. As soon as we know how to lift the mark, we will release the Flaming Sword on her."

I scrunched up my nose. I wasn't entirely sure that I liked being referred to as a weapon.

"I'll come back around for you when it's time to go to the party."

"Wait," I said. "Is there anything I should or shouldn't do?"

"Besides pretending that you're not in love with the commander? Pretend that you want to be a part of this academy and, of course, praying wouldn't hurt."

The door closed, and immediately Remy went on a tirade on how she better be out of this hellhole in a week, or she was kidnapping Trev's brother and having her way with him.

I tuned her out as I headed toward the shower in my room. Closing the bathroom door behind me I stared at the reflection in my mirror. I was tired and the dark circles that appeared under my blue eyes was just confirmation to my exhaustion. My brown hair that was normally shiny hung in greasy waves down my back. I gripped the counter for one last second before I took the quickest shower ever. I needed time to mentally prepare because I needed this night to go smoothly. I needed to do the right thing. And I really needed to see Finn.

eight

DRESSED IN THE PLAIN BLACK dress and matching flats, I waited on Trev to come and escort me to the party. Remy was pacing in front of the bed. Her black hair swinging around her chin as she pivoted to stalk back in front of me again for the hundredth time.

"What is it, Remy?"

She slapped a hand on her tight jeans. "I can't explain it, but I feel like something terrible is going to happen tonight."

"Well, I mean, it is possible."

"Don't joke." She stopped pacing and came to stand right in front of me. "I want our own plan. If something goes sideways tonight, you run, and I'll hold them off for as long as I can."

I pulled her in for a hug. "We are going to be just fine."

"What is with you and all these hugs? Is it just me, or have you become uber needy?" And just like that, my strong friend was back in place. "Of course we're going to be fine. I'm a ghost. Like, who is going to get one up on me? And you're slightly less cool, but still! We are a dynamite team."

She was so nervous I wanted to hug her again, but I was afraid she would hit me.

There was a knock on the door, saving me from doing so. After Remy disappeared, I opened it to find Trev looking dashing in a gray tuxedo. He was pulling on his tie as he ran his eyes over my body.

"Even in a plain, potato-sack-looking dress, you still look beautiful."

"Thank you. Did you find the info you were looking for?"

"Yes and no, but it's a start. I need to explain some things before we go to the party, but I can't spend more than a few minutes in your room."

I rolled my eyes. "Are you serious? The headmistress cares about being improper?"

"Hardly," he said. "But there are eyes everywhere, and if it looks as if we are giving you too much time and attention, then the headmistress will question our loyalties. I will be able to explain some things to you throughout the night. Ezra and Luna have also been assigned to you. They will be your guards tonight, and what I don't have time to explain, they will."

We stepped out into the hall with the familiar coldness nipping at my heels.

Trev's lips curled into a smile. "Glad you're coming with us, Remy. Just remember, there are also ears everywhere."

She didn't respond, but we knew that she understood. Nowhere in this academy was safe.

He held out his arm and escorted me out of my new room. He was right; I immediately felt eyes on me.

Tilting my chin up, I walked with my bandaged hand down by my side, gripping Trev's hand with my other hand. He was giving the perfect image of a good little soldier escorting a pawn to a party.

As we went down three flights of steps to the main level, I took in the building. The Academy of Seraph was grander, with its sprawling estate and brick buildings. It reeked of money and serenity. This was the opposite. It had more of a modern feel. From the looks of the peeling wallpaper to the wobbly banister, the building required some tender loving care. Even though the Academy of the Seraph was older and more pristine, this building looked like no one was even trying to maintain it.

Trev's body language had changed the moment we had exited our small corridor. His face no longer wore a smile, but he acted like the soldier that he was supposed to be.

From the side of his mouth, he said, "We have one building, not multiple. But the building has ten levels, not including the three dungeon levels. There are two exits on each level."

I knew the reason he was giving me the breakdown of the school's layout was not for idle chitchat. It was in case tonight went sideways.

His brother stood in the hallway with a small group of girls gathered around him, to which he ignored all. Noticing us approach, he jerked his head toward a door to his right.

Trev drew his brows together before he yanked me to a stop right in front of a group of students. Loudly, he said, "Seriously? You need to go to the bathroom again? You must have the smallest bladder in the world."

Um … Say what?

"You have two minutes. Don't make me come in after you."

He winked at the group of kids who were laughing at me and my, apparently, freakishly small bladder. Then he pushed me toward a communal bathroom, which I entered on high alert. Whatever the hell Trev had up his sleeve might not necessarily be to my benefit.

A long-legged girl with cotton candy pink hair and big blue eyes came out of a stall. She was gorgeous. One of those girls who you look at and immediately underestimate. If you just passed her on the street, you would think she was heading to a ballet class, but if you met her eyes, you would know that this girl had more than just pointe shoes on her mind. Cold air danced all around me as this girl walked right up to me. Her blue eyes took in my measure as they skimmed over every inch of me as if she was trying to take in my worth.

As she crowded me, I tilted my chin up. "So, do I pass?"

A smile graced her pretty face. "I think me and you will get along just fine. I'm Luna, by the way." She reached behind me and flipped the lock. "We don't have much time. I just found out that tonight's party will be a little different, and Ezra thought it was best that I talked to you before you go walking blindly into a stressful situation. We don't have time for a history lesson, so here is the short version. The Academy of Seraph uses demis and fully blessed to help them fight their battles with demons. Camaella, the right-hand commander to Lucifer, uses demons. Everyone thinks that the headmistress uses demons, too, but that is false information, leaked by the headmistress herself."

"What does she use?"

"Wendigos."

I scrunched my eyebrows together. "I know that this should mean something to me, but I—"

"Lessons later. The important part is that, when they call a wendigo forward tonight, you don't make eye contact. Keep quiet and try to stay hidden. The chances of it actually picking you are slim to none, especially since they go after power and, thanks to Ezra, it'll look like you have none. Plus, saying you're the commander's soulmate was not only a nice touch, but it pretty much creates immunity for you." Her eyes darted toward the door. "Time is up. Do not ask any questions about this to Trev because—"

"There are eyes everywhere," I finished.

She nodded. "Fast learner." She unlocked the door. "Remember, no eye contact and stick by the brothers or my side at all times. You go out first."

"Thank you," I said.

She gave me a wink. "I hope you bring this house down."

I exited the bathroom to cheering. The students who had been snickering were now surrounding Trev, who had started the applause.

I took a bow.

"Jeez," he said, "What took so long?"

"There was someone else in there," I whined, "and I'm a shy pee-er."

He rolled his eyes dramatically for the benefit of the students. "Well, if you are done wasting my time, let me escort you to the party."

Coldness surrounded me, which was a good indicator of how nervous Remy was.

I didn't breathe a word of what Luna had said to me. I remained quiet as we passed some more students out in the hall.

As we took a left down the narrow hall, I asked, "Why are we passing so many students? Is the party just for seniors?"

He clenched his jaw. "Apparently, tonight is a different sort of gathering, in which it would be only for the most promising students, along with all teachers and faculty."

I wiped a hand down my dress. The look on his face, with Remy's premonition, had me sweating.

He stopped before two huge, golden doors. Before he opened them, however, he leaned down and whispered into my ear, "Show no emotion. None. If you do, we're screwed."

I steeled myself and said a silent prayer that whatever was behind those doors allowed me to keep a façade of being calm. I thought of the tiny boy in the cell. I couldn't blow it. He needed out.

nine

IT WASN'T THE FACT THAT I was behind enemy lines and was going to attend a party hosted by a freaking maniac that shook me. It was the fact that I wasn't expecting the sight before me.

Music blared from the sound system, and it wasn't by a well-known composer, but lyrics spouted from a famous rapper who had recently passed away. The lights were turned down low as a strobe light pulsated to the beat. It caused my eyes to strain and would more than likely give me a bigger headache than the one that I was currently sporting. There were almost a hundred students and faculty gathered in a not so large space that was nowhere as big or nice as the gymnasium back at the Academy of Seraph.

Trev steered me around the crowd and toward the back of the room. Once I got up close, I could see that the

wallpaper was peeling in the corners here, too, and the floors had deep grooves and scratches in them, making my shoes skid on the worn-out floor. The furniture scattered here and there looked like yard sale finds, so who knew if the academy was monetarily struggling, but my guess would have been a sound yes.

"Low on funds?"

"Well, the headmistress can't create money."

I jerked my head toward his as I tried my hardest to blend in with the wallpaper. "What's that supposed to mean?"

He whispered in my ear, "The commander can create illusions to where things look like money, or the people believe that it is money. Not sure. I've never seen him do it, but I know that is how his school is so well-funded. The headmistress, even with Thalan, is not as strong as the commander."

Wow. Finn could create money? That was a pretty neat trick to have. I mean, the world was quickly turning to shit, so I wasn't positive that trick would come in handy in the future, but then again, what did I know? I was a newbie at all this.

The headmistress went up a small riser to a narrow platform where an actual DJ stood. The lights around his table illuminated her as she strutted toward him. I had never been to a club, but between the sticky floors and the smell of sweat, I was pretty sure I hadn't missed out on much.

The headmistress gripped a chair that the DJ handed her then climbed up on it and shook her whiskey glass. She had changed into a short dress that was just as sheer as her long one. The bloodred color matched her lips.

"We party here tonight, under the full moon, to give thanks to the ones who have helped us along the way. We are also having a change of plans. We've decided it's time to pay gratitude. Tonight's sacrifice will be a welcoming one." She smiled brightly. "After all, if we want to remain the best, we must continuously grow our army."

Sacrifice? That woman better be talking about goats.

I looked around the room to gauge everyone's reactions. Trev's fists were clenched beside him, most of the students had stopped smiling, and Ezra, who had been making his way toward us, looked ready for murder.

The headmistress turned slightly to her left while balancing on the chair and nodded at two guards dressed all in black. They both walked toward the left, where a colossal curtain hung from the ceiling. My anxiety went up as they began to pull each side back, and the crowd started shuffling their feet; some with nervous anticipation, and some looked downright fearful.

Once the curtains were pulled back, a glass barrier that ran the entire length of the wall was revealed. The glass was at least eight inches thick. It looked like a shark aquarium, minus the water and sea life. We all stood there, waiting for what, I did not know.

For a moment, the cold air left me, and I knew Remy

would get a closer look at what was behind the glass.

"Don't be shy, love," the headmistress called. "Please, everyone, give her a warm welcome."

Who was she talking about?

Some of the crowd broke out into shouts and cheers, whereas the other half looked like they were a turtle trying to hide in their shell. Whatever was behind the glass wall, the room was divided on how they felt about it.

A minute later, a monster that one could only imagine in their nightmares flew at the glass. It was over six feet tall but so skinny that its ribs were protruding. Its ashen body was so pale that I bet, if the lights were on, you could see its veins, and it was completely hairless. A long, black nail made a screeching sound on the glass as it paced in front of its audience. When its black eyes searched the crowd, I immediately remembered Luna's words and cast my eyes downward, staring at the parquet floor.

Ezra joined us against the wall. Trev had taken a step in front of me while his brother covered my other half.

Ezra whispered, "Who is she pointing at?"

How did they even know that that being was a *she*? It had no lady parts, and it sure as hell better not be pointing at me. My I-no-longer-care tank was past empty. I was running on fumes. Empty. I didn't want any more damn curve balls thrown my way.

Trev tensed beside me as a curse word flew from his lips. My curiosity could take no more. I had to see.

I bent my knees to peer through a small crack between

the brothers. The crowd had parted, and there was no mistaking that the wendigo was pointing at a girl who stood alone, as everyone started to back away from her like she carried the plague. That cotton candy pink hair, I would recognize anywhere. Luna.

The same two guards who had pulled back the curtain to showcase the wendigo approached her. They grabbed her arms and started to pull her through the parted crowd. Her head was down as she snarled at them both like a rabid wolf. Light pink hair flew around her shoulders as she bucked against her captors, and when she finally connected with one of her guards in a head butt, she tilted her head back in laughter. She met the brothers' eyes and, for a moment, she quit fighting the brutes who were dragging her. Then the moment was over, and she was back to being a hellcat.

I was getting a sick feeling, understanding what the headmistress had meant when she had said *sacrifice*, and I also knew this girl wasn't a willing participant.

Ezra balled his fists. "What are we going to do?"

Trev shook his head. "We knew, at some point, it would be one of us."

Ezra shifted his weight onto the balls of his feet like he was ready to pounce. Trev, on the other hand, hadn't moved an inch since Luna had been dragged up the riser steps to stand before the headmistress, who was giving Luna a malicious smile. I had so many damn questions.

"We don't know how the wendigo makes its choice," the

headmistress started, "but it is clear that the choice has been made. The wendigo desires our dear Luna."

The crowd started applauding, while the headmistress leaned forward and whispered something into Luna's ear, making the girl go pale. The guards then dragged the hellcat down the steps and tied her to a chair directly in front of the glass wall.

Trev backed us into a corner. "We can't let the wendigo have her. If it were one of us tied to that chair, she would be breaking necks."

"We need a plan," Ezra said, "and it will have to be a damn good one, or we are all dead."

The cold air had returned and swirled around the three of us, letting us know that Remy was back. We couldn't see her, but that didn't mean we couldn't hear her.

"That is exactly what the hell I have been saying all this time. I swear you two are hot. Like some good genes run in your family. Congrats on your faces, but seriously, is there a freaking brain between the two of you?"

Ezra jumped almost a foot as he looked around. "What did I just hear?"

"That's a friend of Gabriella's," Trev informed him.

"Hello, hot stuff," Remy said.

Ezra's eyes grew round. "Am I hearing a ghost?"

I was squished between both brothers, my arms touching them. "Yes, if I touch you and wish you to see her, then you can. I can't see her with my powers bound, so I'm assuming that you both can't see her either. Apparently, however, I'm still somehow allowing you both to hear her."

I rubbed my forehead. It could be that my body was trying to shed this binding naturally.

"Just wanted to clarify that we're talking about a ghost, correct?" Trev asked.

Remy sighed. "Why are the pretty ones always so dumb?"

When an older gentleman, closer to us in the back, turned to look at us, out of the side of my mouth, I said, "Hush."

Ezra was mumbling to himself about uncanny powers, making Remy laugh. They were so going to get us caught.

Once Luna was restrained with some sort of cuffs that made her hiss, the guards stepped back.

Ezra said in a low voice. "The wendigo will be released at the end of the party, when the clock strikes midnight."

The crowd was loud, so I was praying no one heard us.

"What happens when that thing is released?"

Trev said, "It will either kill her if it thinks her powers aren't grand enough or turn her into a wendigo if it deems her worthy."

I didn't know about Luna, but I would go with option one if I had a choice.

"Well, boys, what are you thinking?"

"We need to come up with something quick," Ezra said.

"The problem is, if we rescue her, what will it be for?" Trev questioned.

While everyone's attention was enamored with the beast

that was stalking its glass enclosure, now was the perfect time for me to ask a few questions.

"Explain," I said.

"We are all marked, remember? We can't leave here without permission. So, if I betray the headmistress by saving Luna, then what? None of us, other than you and Remy, can leave."

"So, we really need to kill the one that put the marks on all of you to begin with?" I asked.

"Yeah, and Trev got a hint of who that person was today," Ezra said.

"Thalan?"

They both scoffed.

"No, we wish," Trev said. "If that was the case, we would have all been freed long ago."

"So, who do we have to kill?" Remy asked.

That's my girl. Loyal should have been her middle name.

"I talked with Thalan today," Trev said. "Since I am the head of the headmistress's guards, he was cluing me in on their plan of action. He said that the most powerful of wendigos, the original, isn't allowed to make an appearance because she's too valuable. He said that she is the one that put the mark on—" He stopped talking as a young drunk guy walked in front of us. Then he resumed. "This powerful wendigo is the one that marks us."

Man, my head was throbbing. "How do you get your marks?"

"It's a serum that is injected. Then our mark appears."

If everyone here had a mark that tied them to this academy and there was no chance of escaping, they would have to stay and fight to the death.

I looked around at the crowded bodies. There was no way we would make it out of here alive. For a greater cause, we either let Luna die to keep our mission a secret, essentially saving many others, or we bring out the big guns.

"Unbind my powers," I whispered. My gut was telling me that now was the time.

"Thalan will know that you are more than we are pretending you to be," Trev said.

"Maybe I am more than you think that I am."

The brothers exchanged a look over my head while Remy whispered, "Burn this mother down."

"How close does this Thalan have to be in order to sense what I'm capable of?"

Ezra shrugged. "Two feet? He can't pick up on anyone's powers from a distance; that's for sure."

I nodded. *Good.* We could work with that.

The wendigo was ramming into the glass, causing several people to jump back from the partition. Others who felt more secure taunted the wendigo.

"So," Remy said, "is there just the one behind the glass?"

Trev tilted his head toward the pacing wendigo. "Behind the glass wall, there is a pit that remains closed. The headmistress opens it when she wants to allow one wendigo out for sacrificial purposes. Down the pit is where all the wendigos live. It's like a plane that is neither here nor there."

Ezra said, "We need someone who has, um ... been extra blessed by the angels."

I knew that no one other than the archangels, Finn, and my best friends knew about me being blessed by multiple angels, so he could only be talking about the Flaming Sword.

I pinched Trev's back, making him flinch. "Oh, and you just thought I would be the girl who would go behind the wall, down into the pit, and kill the queen of scary-ass wendigos?"

"You are our only hope," Ezra said. "Plus, we didn't find out until recently who or what put the mark on everyone. And that what? It just happens to be down in the pit?"

"Um, how about hell to the no," Remy said. "Crawling into pits housed by wendigos to kill the boss of those things? That's going to be a hard no."

"She can do it." Trev looked at me. "I know you can."

Maybe he was right. Would Uriel, someone who supposedly loved me like an uncle, come to me and lie to me if he thought it would get me killed? Would the other archangels, including my own mother, not try to steer me from this path if they felt that I couldn't ride out the journey? There was no doubt in my mind that Uriel was telling me that this might not be the path I would have chosen, but it was a path my conscience could handle. Chamuel had said that everyone needed me. This was what I was born to do—help those who needed it the most.

"Here is what we are going to do." I didn't know why I was taking charge, but here I was, laying it out. "Bring Thalan over here. Let's get the greetings over with. Then unbind my powers. We will do our best to dodge Thalan while we are here. We have three hours to come up with a plan."

"If the headmistress realizes what we are up to, then we are done for," Trev warned.

"Speak for yourself, pretty boy," Remy said from somewhere in front of me.

Ezra chuckled. "Pretty boy, huh?"

"Yeah, Trev's the Liam to your Chris, Mr. Hemsworth."

"So, basically, you're saying I'm the hotter brother," Ezra stated.

Through my teeth, I gritted out, "Children, right now is not the time for a beauty contest. And while I'm on it—"

The headmistress interrupted me by having the DJ turn down the music while, once again, she climbed back on her chair. She tapped on her glass and cleared her throat before saying, "One last thing before I let you get back to the party. If you all will take a look at the back wall, our lovely Gabriella, the one looking as if she would rather be anywhere other than here, has come to join our ranks."

I gave a finger wave to numerous faces currently staring at me. I didn't have it in me to smile.

"Gabriella," the headmistress continued, "is going to lure the commander to us."

A stout man with rolls under his neck who was directly

in front of the risers said, "The commander would never willingly give us something that could kill him."

The headmistress glared at him. "Yes, I'm aware. But it seems as if our Gabriella has a special hold over the commander, and she has agreed to become a darken."

The man scoffed. "Are you just going to lure him here, hoping he won't slaughter all of us in the process?"

Ooo ... The headmistress was getting mad now. "No, Gerald, I am not." Her eyes found the three of us in the back. "I'm not stupid. After we take care of dear Luna here, we will have Gabriella take on the mark, binding her here to the academy. If the commander wants his alleged soulmate back, he will either tell us where the Flaming Sword is, or he'll have to kill the one who allowed us to put the mark on her in the first place. The ones of us who are privy to that information"—she gave him a pointed look—"should know that in itself is an impossible feat. Regardless, if I can just get him close enough to the academy, none of this will matter."

Questions were being asked, but I tuned all of them out. Why would she need Finn close to the academy? She's no match for him. If she thought to put a mark on Finn, she was crazy. He would never allow that, and there was no way in hell I was going to be permanently stuck on this campus.

The headmistress put a hand up in the air and halted all talk. "Enough. We came here to celebrate another month gone and"—she cut her eyes to Luna—"to have a sacrifice. Eat, drink, and prepare yourself for a night to remember."

Cold air whipped around me. "What are we going to do?"

From the side of my mouth, I said, "First, we save Luna. Now get Thalan over here."

The music was turned back up to ear-bursting levels while the lights flashed to the pulsating beat. I cradled my bandaged hand to my chest, not because it hurt but because I was literally about to have a panic attack. I felt like I kept trying to beat a level of Jumanji only to have someone roll the dice yet again.

As Trev leaned up against the back wall, the cold air would weave in agitation between us every once and a while.

A few minutes later, Ezra brought Thalan to stand in front of me. The headmistress was hot on their trail.

"Thalan," Trev started, "I'd like to introduce you to Gabriella and for you to see if there is anything that we missed that might help us against the commander."

The man was reed-thin and stood a few inches shorter than Trev. His black hair was slicked back from his face, showcasing an oily forehead and hawkish nose. His thin lips peeled back as he showed his disgust over me.

"Boys, I don't know what it is you expect me to see, other than a waste of being blessed. She must be a low-level demi." Then he gave me a disdainful look. "Enjoy the party tonight, darken, because you will not be invited to any more. Only the intermediate powers and up get the privilege."

He said this like I should be ashamed of not being invited to a shindig where a freaking wendigo nominates one person to convert or slaughter. It took everything I had not to roll my eyes, but as my left eye started to twitch, I figured I was starting to lose that battle.

The thin man shivered. "Is it cold in here, or is it just me?"

The headmistress tilted her head to the side as she studied me. "Well, it looks as if the only thing our Gabriella is good for is snaring the commander." She chuckled. "Soulmate." As she dismissed me for the below-average demi that she thought me to be, she grabbed the trail of her dress and spun around. "Come on, Thalan; let us mingle."

Remy whispered, "This party blows."

Then Ezra whispered, "When I unbind your powers, you might feel like you want to pass out. Don't."

"Good advice, oh wise one," I snarked.

He jerked his head toward a small door behind the DJ booth. "That is where the kitchens are. Head that way, pretending to look for a bathroom. I'll be on your heels."

I sighed. All these clandestine meetings were falling under the pretense that my bladder is weak, but I guess it could be worse.

I walked hurriedly toward the kitchens. And as soon as I made it inside the door, a hand was laid upon me from behind, steering me into a cooler where herbs were kept.

"We must hurry," Ezra said. "It's going to be painful but try to relax."

I gave him a what-the-hell look. "Why would you even

85

say that?"

He shrugged. "Pep talks aren't really my thing."

"So, just say nothing."

He stared at me blankly for a few seconds until I groaned. I had way too many smartasses in my life.

"Okay. Get on with it."

With his huge hands, he grabbed either side of my head. Heat swirled from his palms that would have made me sweat if we weren't in an icy cooler. My knees almost buckled, but the pressure he had on my head kept me upright.

"Stay with me," he commanded.

"Trying," I gritted out.

It might have been seconds or minutes later, but I found myself on my knees with sweat dripping off my forehead and onto the cement of the freezer floor. My vision darkened. Power swirled back to me stronger than I ever recalled. It must have been building even with the bind around my mind.

"I'd like to give you time to recoup, but we don't have any," he said, his voice sounding so far away. "Let me help you to your feet and get you back out there."

I felt like my intestines had been jerked out of my body, reorganized, and a toddler had shoved them back in. But I could again feel my bond with Finn, and in that, there was hope.

I was weak now, but I could already feel my body beginning to heal itself. In a few minutes, this academy wouldn't know what hit them.

ten

THE MUSIC WAS BLASTING OUT a rap song about lucid dreams, but my head no longer throbbed as the lyrics pumped out of the speakers. Everyone was dancing and swaying to the music, celebrating the upcoming sacrifice with wine and champagne. They were all so jovial, whether it be because they were sadistic and longed to see a young girl torn apart by a wendigo or because they were happy that it wasn't their necks on the chopping block. I didn't know, nor care. Regardless, I was able to sit on the barstool and catch my breath as I dabbed at the sweat with a bar napkin.

"Are you good?" Ezra asked.

Emotionally? Hell no, I wasn't. I felt like I was dreaming, a very realistic dream. However, physically, I was doing as good as could be expected.

"Peachy."

He gave me a half-smile. "I've got to go talk with my brother. Stay at least a few feet from Thalan."

I waved him away then leaned my elbows back against the bar, watching the crowd. I felt the air around me grow colder as I watched a young male who was bartending as he poured someone a glass of wine. Then I swiveled on my stool to scan the crowd.

I could *feel* Finn. He was so close.

Out of the side of my mouth, I said to the cold air next to me, "I need you to do me a favor. Go as fast as you can and tell Finn to be patient. Tell him, if he storms in here right now, my plan will backfire. Also, tell him that, for some reason, the headmistress wants him close, so he needs to do the opposite. I don't want him anywhere near those lavender fields."

Remy's voice was barely above a whisper when she replied, "Glad someone has a freaking plan. Is it just me, or is this like a total shitshow?"

"Tell him that they will try to harm me to get to him. Give me three hours, and then he can storm the damn gates."

"I don't want to leave you."

The bartender came closer, grabbed a rag, and then turned back to the other side.

"I know."

"Can you feel him? Is he close?"

I slightly nodded. "I can feel him. That's why I'm worried. He is in sight of this school. He needs to back away. I can feel his anger and his bloodlust. He knows that I can feel him, and he's waiting for a sign, but not patiently, so please go and hurry back."

She sighed, but she did as I asked.

It took an hour before my friend returned. When she came over to me, the bar was now crowded, so I evacuated my seat and found us a corner near the golden doors. Waiting a few minutes to make sure that no one watched me, I asked her what had happened.

She didn't answer right away, causing my anxiety to rise. "Remy ..."

She sighed. "Did Trev or his hot-ass brother talk to you?"

I looked around for the brothers who were currently missing from my eyesight. "Um ... no. About what?"

She hesitated before saying, "I couldn't find the commander."

Impossible. I felt him.

"So, where did Richard and Dan say he had gone? Did you see Hannah?"

"Nope. Didn't see any of them."

My powers thrummed inside of me. She was lying.

"Remy, what is going on?"

"Shh ... They'll hear us," she said as students started coming closer to our hideout. "You know we are all going to be stuck at this damn academy, right?"

I watched the headmistress twirl around with a portly fellow. "Maybe. Maybe not. But why are you saying that now?"

"I'll be back," Remy said.

"Wait."

But it was too late. She was already gone.

What the heck was Remy up to? I knew that Finn was alive and not hurt, because I could feel him. He was so close, rage and hunger burning through him. He was agitated and close, but where was he?

eleven

TREV GRABBED AHOLD OF MY elbow. "Did you eat any of the candy in the bowls?"

I staggered to the left, making him almost scoop me up from the floor. A few people laughed as I giggled.

"Whoopsie," I said.

"Yeah, *whoopsie.* I should have told you, but I've been a little distracted trying to converse with Thalan so he doesn't get too close to you."

I stumbled again.

"That wasn't real candy. You'll be hallucinating in no time. Hopefully, with your uncanny powers, you will burn through the drug relatively fast, but for the next fifteen minutes, at least, you're going to be riding dragons and seeing purple elephants."

"Elephants!" I squealed. "Oh em gee, they are my

favorite animal. So damn loyal, they are. Super stoked about that. Don't know about dragons, though. Am I flame retardant?"

He shook his head and sighed.

As Trev steered me through the crowd, I looked for the headmistress, but she was nowhere in sight.

I dug in my heels and whispered, "I got to go find Finn."

"Nope. You need water." He was talking to someone while I swayed my hips to the music.

Someone pushed me down in a chair, and then I heard Ezra's deep voice. "She needs to sleep. She'll heal faster."

"We are kind of on a time crunch," Remy said.

I slurred, "Oh, hey, bestie who is hiding a secret. Would you like to share with the class? I know you're lying, so spill it. You know I could just try to sift through your thoughts; pluck them from that brain of yours."

"Shit," Ezra said. "Try to block my body."

A warm hand covered my spinning head. The heat from their palm made me sigh right before the world turned dark.

I had to be dream walking. I felt someone pulling me toward them. I swear, if it was that witch, Camaella, I was going to ball up in a fetal position and cry for my archangel mommy. That had me laughing as the dream began to grow clearer.

I walked across a meadow to the familiar archangel. Sandalphon sat on a rock near a creek bed. The muddy water flowed down the stream behind him, and the sun was shining on his blond hair, making him look every bit the angel that he was. His blue eyes twinkled as I neared.

"Hello, Gabriella."

I didn't understand why I was here. If I could dream walk to anyone, it would have been Finn.

"Not who you wanted to see?" Sandalphon chuckled. "I have been waiting here patiently for you to fall asleep. We need to talk."

I nodded. "Okay. Do you know where Finn is?"

"I do." He stood from the rock. "I need a favor, and then I'll get you through to Finn."

"I don't know if I'm in a position to be doling out favors. I'm kind of in the middle of a shitshow right now."

He chuckled. "I'm well-aware. I heard my brother, Uriel, talked with you?"

I nodded. "I also got to talk to the seven who are now … you know." I pointed up to the heavens.

He smiled. "I heard that, as well. I'm glad you got to visit them. My brothers and sisters are big on not giving out too much information at one time."

I snickered. "Yeah, I kind of noticed."

"It's actually for an excellent reason. One slight alter of a plan could change your future. According to Haniel, your future could be amazing, so none of us want to rob you of that. Normally, I wouldn't interfere, but I'm worried."

He rubbed a hand on the back of his neck. It was such a human thing to do that I smiled.

"What can I help you with?"

"I watched you grow, and my love for you is immeasurable, just like it is for another child that I watched grow. Finn is like my own son. He needed more love than you did, though. You had a wonderful mother, along with a horde of aunts and uncles who loved you. Finn's life was hard with having the father that he does. In all sense of the word, he is mine."

All of a sudden, I had a pit in my stomach. "Is something wrong with Finn?"

"He is … hurt."

I clenched my fists. I had known something was wrong when I could feel him nearby, but Remy claimed she couldn't find him. "But he is immortal."

"He isn't dying."

I breathed a sigh of relief. "Tell me where he is."

He nodded. "I'll send you to him right now, but first, Gabriella, the favor I need of you is to try your hardest not to kill any wendigos. You'll have many opportunities, but if you kill them, I can promise that you will regret it."

I started to ask what the heck I was supposed to do with the wendigos—play patty-cake with them?—but before I could ask, I felt this tug in my stomach, as if something was trying to pull me away from Sandalphon.

He frowned. "Someone is trying to wake you up. I want you to see my boy. Go now."

He pushed both hands toward me, and a massive amount of energy hit me, sending me flying to a different time and place.

I twirled around until my eyes landed on him.

Finn stood in front of me in a field of lavender flowers. His black hair was in stark contrast to his eyes, those damn eyes. Green jewels pierced mine. His hands were in his pockets as he half-stood with his feet braced apart. He had on black cargo pants, and the T-shirt that he wore was pulled so taut I could see his pec muscles as he crossed his arms.

My heart raced as I grew closer. He was magnificent.

I heard the rumble from his chest as laughter bubbled from his lips. "Thoughts, Maka, I can hear your thoughts."

I ran toward him. "Don't care."

Right before I flung myself toward him, he took two steps backward.

"Gabriella, baby ..." He held both hands out in front of him.

"What the hell kind of greeting is that?"

He wouldn't make eye contact as he said, "I'm not sure if I should touch you."

"Why?" I was feeling the tug in my stomach again. Aggravation at whoever was trying to wake me made me shout, "Finn, why are you acting so weird?"

I took a step toward him and grabbed his wrist. His eyes looked horrified for a second before his body relaxed.

"Finn, what are you doing in a field? A field that I don't

recognize. I thought you were close to the Empowered Academy."

He shrugged. "I was."

Something was very wrong. Finn looked at me with such sorrow, a longing on his face that was tearing my heart into pieces.

"Finn, talk to me."

"Something happened, Gabriella."

"Like …?" I tried to lighten the situation. "If you tell me that you went and got yourself captured while I was back at the bar hallucinating, I'll flip the hell out."

A small smile curved his lips. "No one could contain me, Maka. I'll find my way back to you."

"What does that mean? Where the hell are you, Finn?"

He put a piece of my hair behind my ear oh so gently. Then, cupping my chin, he leaned down and kissed me. I threw myself into his arms, and he tangled his hand in my hair, lightly jerking my head back, exposing me more to him as he settled his lips on mine. The kiss ended way too quickly for my liking.

With his eyes, he scanned over my face, landing briefly on my bandaged hand before he pulled me in for another hug. Finn's warm breath whispered against the shell of my ear, sending shivers down my body. "You do realize that I am going to kill Trev, right?"

"He really had to obey the headmistress. There was no other way. Besides, my fingers are currently in the process of healing back, thanks to Raphael's gift. Cool, right?"

"Maka, the things you get yourself into."

This wasn't the time to smile, but Lord help me, I couldn't stop my lips from curving upward.

I pulled back from him a little and gave him a watery smile. "I dreamed of you, and that day, you know."

He looked saddened for a second. "You don't have much time. I can feel you slipping away from me, and we need to talk about something very important. Two things can kill a wendigo—another wendigo and the Flaming Sword. Their souls are trapped in beastly bodies, living every day over and over. The fallen, the archangels, nor the fully blessed are capable of killing a wendigo. They can be sent to hell and trapped there, but they don't die."

Why was he telling me all of this?

Someone was shaking me awake. I gripped his forearms so that I could stay with him, but this time the tug was too strong.

As I was quickly disappearing from him, I heard him whisper, "I'll find my way back to you."

twelve

I CAME AWAKE WITH A start. Two faces were staring at me with concern, but I ignored both brothers and the cold air that was pressing into the chair with me. I looked around the dim room where bodies still gyrated to the loud music. I could smell the sweat from here. My hand itched under the bandage where my fingers were regenerating.

"Do either of you know where Finn is?"

The brothers both were too quick to say, "No."

I raised my eyebrows. "First, Remy lied, and now both of you? If you know where he is, I need to know. Something isn't right. I can feel him, but I can't see him."

Trev laid a hand on my shoulder. "We will find him together, I promise. For right now, can we focus on Luna? She has fifteen minutes before the wendigo is to be set upon her. Besides, I can swear to you that I don't know exactly where Finn is."

Now I narrowed my eyes. "But you have an idea."

Ezra cleared his throat. "We do, but we're probably wrong. We need to know for certain. The headmistress left during the party, and she isn't back yet, which makes no sense. We overheard a guard saying the headmistress let out thirty wendigos right before the party, so maybe she went to check on them?"

"Why would she let out such a vast amount of wendigos?" I asked.

"We can't focus on where she went and why right now," Trev said. "We have a problem."

"Like bigger than the one that we're currently facing?" I asked.

"Sort of," Remy answered. "The headmistress disappearing while you were out is a big deal. The brothers said that she must remain within certain distances from the wendigos in order to control them."

Ezra added, "The word is the headmistress came across some intel regarding the commander."

My stomach tightened. What had Finn gotten himself into?

Remy whispered, "Tick, tock. Luna is one dead chicken in fourteen."

"It's crowded and dark in here," I said. "I need one of you to get me close to Luna. I have to tell her of my plan, or this will backfire."

Trev asked no questions. Instead, he helped me stand.

"You'll need to act still wasted," he whispered. Then he steered a wobbly me toward where Luna was strapped down.

Her blue eyes were blazing with fury at anyone who got too close to her, but when she saw me approaching, she shook her head. "Don't do anything stupid."

"Don't worry," I said. "We're still going to leave you strapped down."

"Um … well, if this is a rescue attempt, you guys suck at it."

As I looked at Luna, I knew what to do. Chamuel was right; my gut wouldn't lead me astray.

Tugging my arm out of Trev's grasp, I pretended to stumble as I caught myself using Luna. "Forgive me for not asking," I whispered as I slammed my palm against the center of her chest.

She hissed before her eyes rolled back into her head.

I quickly straightened. The only persons who noticed my fall were a few students dancing nearby and Thalan. Of course. He narrowed his eyes as he took me in. Before the end of the night, he would question me again, which would be a huge problem.

Luna's chin was on her chest, looking dead to the world, but I could see the rise and fall of her chest. I sent up a silent prayer that everything would work out as I moved drunkenly toward the dance floor.

"She will not die tonight," I announced.

Trev was super confused, but he nodded, taking me at my word. I could tell that he wanted to ask me what the hell all that was about, but he didn't. Smart boy. Until he told me where he thought Finn could be, I wasn't having share time.

The fluorescent lights were in sync with the bass of the music that was thumping out from the speakers. Continuing with my inebriated state, I skirted to the outside of the group where I came upon Thalan, again. He was still staring at me warily.

I had to ask the brothers, "If we can't take out the headmistress, and I can't kill the wendigos—"

"What?" both boys interrupted.

I nodded as Thalan began to move off the wall and toward us. "No time to explain. He will know about me soon, and we can't let that happen." Ezra came up beside me while Trev followed behind. "Back him in a corner. I have some questions."

Without hesitation, both brothers crowded in on Thalan, whose mouth opened and closed like a bass just waiting to get hooked. Then his eyes widened when I stood a foot before him.

Both brothers were now crowding into my back, blocking Thalan and me from the crowd.

"You are more than you say you are. You are *extremely* blessed."

"Aw … Thanks, boo. Now that you know that I'm more than I seem, let me ask you how we can call up the original?"

He didn't answer, but he didn't need to. I got the

information from him. As soon as I asked the question, he immediately thought of the answer, even as he shook his head. I also got flooded with an onslaught of images that I didn't want to see.

This man was the epitome of evil. He killed with barely a thought. Women and children meant nothing to him. His soul was black.

He tilted his chin in the air. "I'm not telling you. All I need to do is yell, and the headmistress will have your head on a platter before the end of the night. I have personally killed thousands of—"

I laid a palm on his chest and concentrated on the energy that I wanted to call forth. It was different from what I gave Luna. This wasn't pure. This power was scary. It was dark and powerful.

My palm lit up for a split-second before Thalan took his last breath and crumpled to the floor, looking like a drunken sack.

"Leave him," I said. "What's the point of trying to hide a body when this whole thing is about to turn into a chaotic mess?"

Trev gave me a questioning look. "At least he's in a dark corner."

"She wasn't playing about calling her the executioner," Ezra commented.

I should have felt some sort of emotion, other than rage, but I couldn't bring myself to feel remorse for Thalan. He had been a vile man—nothing good left in him—and the world was better off without him.

We went closer to the side of the room that held the aquarium, and the wendigo lunged for the glass, making me jump back a little. Then the wendigo cocked its head at me as it trailed its black nails down the glass.

Trev nudged me forward. "Just to circle back to your last comment … If you don't kill the wendigo, it will touch others here. That means that everyone in this room who can't escape will either turn into a wendigo or die. Keep that in mind."

"I know. I'm hoping I can just disable the wendigo." I wasn't exactly sure what I was capable of. "One little hitch to the plan is the original wendigo can't be summoned. The headmistress goes into the portal when she needs something from them."

Both brothers mumbled several expletives.

The look on Trev's face said he thought he was going to die tonight, but he was in it to win it. Ezra looked just as defeated, but the devil-may-care look was his staple, so I might have misread him.

The binding around my heart tightened. I didn't understand it. Finn was so close, but where? As we walked farther away from where Thalan's body was, I turned around, ignoring the wendigo at my back as I scanned the crowd for Finn.

The DJ's cheery voice rumbled over the speakers. He killed the music then asked for everyone to assemble in front of the offering table.

We moved away from the enclosure. Ezra came up beside his brother. Cold air hovered near us.

"Remy, stay hidden," I said. "Things are about to get real."

"Aye, aye, Captain," she whispered with humor in her voice.

At midnight, the guards flipped a lever then hit a button, causing the glass doors to open. The crowd grew eerily quiet.

The four of us walked closer to where two guards had untied Luna from the chair and were now strapping her down to an altar. Awake once again, she bucked and screamed. However, her strength was no match for the guards who tied to the table within seconds, but only because she wasn't aware of how powerful she was yet. Then the guards slowly backed away from the altar and the approaching wendigo.

"If the headmistress doesn't show up, who does she think will stop the wendigo? Or is that her plan—to kill everyone here?"

"This is the first time this has ever happened. I'm just as confused as you are," Ezra replied.

I shrugged. "I need one of you to make a distraction. The dead guy in the corner would be a good one."

Ezra nodded. "On it."

Trev stepped closer to me. "I'll stay with Gabriella."

Ezra pushed a boy, who had started cheering, out of his way. The boy took one look at Ezra's face and slithered off through the crowd to find a different viewing spot.

As I stalked toward the wendigo, I noticed that it was taking its sweet time, almost as if it was enjoying the attention. Good. The slower, the better.

When I was two feet, I heard a commotion over at the DJ booth, but I didn't dare take my eyes off the wendigo.

Trev whispered, "The headmistress is back. Shouldn't you go after her first?"

I looked over to the risers where the headmistress was. She was standing on her chair again and now had the microphone pressed to her smiling lips.

"I'm sorry that I had to depart for a bit, but something very, very interesting just fell into my lap."

It sure as hell better not have been Finn.

"I had to take care of those matters first." It wasn't my imagination that her eyes narrowed on me for a bit before saying, "Things are definitely getting interesting."

I looked at the approaching wendigo then back to the headmistress, except she was no longer there. "Where did she go?"

"Shit," Trev said. "The headmistress has her wings out. Look above."

I tilted my head back and, sure enough, there she sat on the rafters. Even from this distance, I could see that her eyes were focused between me and the wendigo.

"Do you think she knows about me?"

"No way," Trev said. "Now what?"

I looked over my shoulder to see that Ezra had grabbed

a pretty girl and was flirting with her, pretending that all hell wasn't about to break loose. He must have steered her right to Thalan, because there was a scream that would have made Hollywood proud.

The headmistress's face registered shock as everyone started turning to where the girl was still screaming.

With the wendigo momentarily forgotten, I watched the altar with intensity as it jumped up onto the table, straddling Luna.

Trev clenched his fist.

I put a hand on his arm. "Have faith."

"Let's hope you know what the hell you are doing, Gabriella."

Yeah. Let's hope.

The wendigo took one long, black nail and trailed it down Luna's face. Then it leaned down, and a white smoke uncurled from its mouth. Luna flung her hands up just as the wendigo huddled farther over her. Once its chest touched her palms, it screeched before it fell off the altar and landed on the floor. No one moved as the wendigo started turning into a pool of what looked like crude oil.

Oh shit.

"What just happened?" the headmistress screamed from the rafters.

Everyone started taking a few steps back from the liquified wendigo and the altar.

Luna sat up, visibly shaking as she began to untie her ankles from the straps.

I had just told Sandalphon that I would do my best not to kill any wendigos, and not even thirty minutes later, the remains of a wendigo were coating the cheap floor.

The headmistress flew down from the risers and didn't stop until she was right in front of Luna. "How did you do that?"

A frown was on Luna's beautiful face. "I have no clue what just happened, Headmistress."

The headmistress looked past Luna to me, her eyes narrowed.

Grabbing her attention again, Luna said, "All I know is I didn't kill the wendigo."

"Ma'am?" the guard closest to her said. "We can't explain how Thalan died. Until we know for certain, we should clear the area."

The headmistress pointed at Luna. "Don't think you escaped the sacrifice."

Guards quickly surrounded her, and I lost any opportunity to wield the Flaming Sword on her. There was no way I could take on all of them, not until I figured out my powers' limitations.

Luna nodded as she headed toward us. However, Trev gave her a shake of his head, and she veered off in a different direction. That was a good call. We couldn't afford to draw any more attention to us.

The students and faculty were quickly clearing out, but I dragged my heels as the headmistress shouted at one of the guards, "Did you break her yet?"

"Not yet," one of the guards said.

"What do you mean *not yet*?"

"We are working on it," the guard answered.

I pretended not to listen as we slowly shuffled our way to the door, but the sickening groan, followed by something hitting the floor, clued me in that the headmistress had just minimized her staff.

"And you," she screeched, "have we found out what went wrong today? None of the commander's people were slaughtered! None. The wendigo was supposed to kill all of his people. Instead, when we made it down to the ridge, there was nothing but a ton of oil matching what is similar to *that*"—she pointed at the remains of the wendigo that Luna had killed—"coating the forest before the lavender fields, and now we have proof of what that oil represents. Someone tell me how this is possible."

"Perhaps he has the Flaming Sword?" a guard suggested.

"And what? Does Luna also have the Flaming Sword hidden somewhere on her person?"

There was silence from the guards as Trev picked up the pace, and I matched him.

This didn't make sense. While the headmistress still yelled at her guards, my power coiled around me, squeezing me like a python. When I didn't fight the power surge, it uncoiled like a violent serpent that had been waiting for the perfect moment to strike.

Trev was looking at me strangely as he tugged me along, but it was too late. My gift of power from Haniel had snatched on to the headmistress's thoughts. Without even trying, I had plucked at her brain, seeking what I wanted … and then my breath hitched as my world began to shake.

The headmistress's words were running on repeat through my mind. The people who Finn had brought … the ones who were right outside of these walls, waiting for me to make my exit, were okay. Yet, there were thirty dead wendigos.

When Trev escorted me back to my room, Remy was there, sitting on my bed in tangible form.

"Something is wrong with her," he said to Remy. Then a look passed between them. "I'll try to find out some more information. When the coast is clear, we will meet in here. Just hang tight." He closed the door behind us.

Not looking at her, I took the bandage off my hand with jerky movements before throwing the gauze into a trash can as I asked, "So, you know where Finn is?"

Her blue eyes filled with tears. "I have a feeling, yes."

She started to say more, but I cut her off, "No, I can't right now."

I stormed off to the bathroom and shed my dress before climbing into the shower. The hot water hit me as I cried until my legs collapsed underneath me.

thirteen

I HAD PUT THE DRESS back on, since that was the only clothes I had, and was sitting on the bed as Remy brushed my hair. I still didn't know where Finn was. He was close, but did that matter anymore? How was I going to help him?

When I had visited him in my dreams, he had told me there were two ways to kill a wendigo. They could die by another wendigo or the Flaming Sword, and until thirty minutes ago, no one held part of the sword in them but me and me alone. Therefore, I knew what Finn had done. He had turned into a wendigo. Still, I didn't know how or why.

I grabbed Remy's hand, making the hairbrush still in my hair. "I need you to go talk to Dan and Richard. I need to know the exact details from their point of view."

She removed the hairbrush. "If it will help your heart,

I will do it."

"Thank you. How fast can you travel?"

"Like the wind. I developed a new trick." She gave me a sad smile. "We will talk about it later."

If I were a good friend, I would stop her and ask her to tell me about her new talent, but all I could think about was needing to know why and how Finn had become one of those creatures. My heart was shattered, but even in the darkness, I wouldn't lose hope or faith. Finn had never given up on me, and I sure as hell wouldn't give up on him.

I was just about to test Haniel's gift again when there was a knock on the door. I didn't bother permitting them to enter, as they were already turning the knob. Then, quickly, Trev, Ezra, and Luna came in. The brothers closed the door then stood off to the side, like they were unsure of what to do. Luna didn't have the same trouble. She climbed up on the bed and threw her arms around me. "I know that you don't really know me," she said, "But my heart is breaking for you. I was eight when I found out that my parents didn't survive a mission that the Headmistress sent them out on. My younger brother died in those cells. The brothers have been sneaking in food to the prisoners since they were little. That is how me and Trev became friends. He would sit on the other side of my cell telling me stories of the outside." I pulled out of her hold so I could search her face. "The Headmistress decided when I was fifteen that I could take my parents place. I work for her because I'm forced to but not one day goes by that I don't think of

my family and what they have endured. I was so broken…
some days I still feel broken. The brother's help me to see
that there is still a fight within me. If I give up on life then
the Headmistress wins. I can't let that happen. Trev told
me what Finn means to you. There could be a possibility
that he's not one of them, you know."

"No, there is no way that he escaped that fate. You can
only kill a wendigo if you are one or possess the Flaming
Sword."

She scoffed. "Well, I'm pretty sure that I somehow killed
that wendigo."

"You did."

She gasped then looked at the brothers, who both
winced. I had a feeling that Luna was going to have their
heads for them not telling her what they already knew.

"Lu," Trev started, "we just put two and two together.
Don't get mad. We thought it best if Gabriella told you
herself."

"What are you guys talking about?" Luna asked.

I wasn't in the mood to do any explaining. But, since
she was three seconds from wigging out, I said, "I'll have
to give you the cliff notes version right now. What I say
stays in this room, or I'll kill all of you myself. Do I make
myself clear?"

Gone was the weak Gabriella. Finn was in trouble and,
from here on out, I would kill anyone who could possibly
be a threat to my well-being. If they got in my way, then I
wouldn't be able to fix this.

When Remy suddenly appeared at the base of the bed, the brothers jumped and Luna's eyes bugged out of her head.

"Did she just teleport?"

Remy gave Luna a funny look. "This ain't *Star Trek*, babe. I'm a ghost."

Luna's mouth dropped open. I waited for her to close it, but when that never happened, I grew impatient.

Ezra gave her a wink. "Nice to meet you in the flesh."

She batted her eyes. "Your pleasure."

Luna was still gaping at Remy, but I had things to do.

"Please focus, everyone. Can all of you keep a secret?"

Finally, Luna nodded. "Of course. I won't tell a soul."

Both brothers agreed, as well, before they looked at Remy.

"Um, I don't know what all of you are looking at"—she gave them a WTF scowl—"but I am the best friend." She clapped her hands together. "I"—*clap*—"already"—*clap*—"know"—*clap*—"her"—*clap*—"secrets."

Taking back over the conversation, I said, "My mother is Gabriel, the archangel." I didn't give them time to ask questions; I simply plowed on ahead. "I have been blessed by eight archangels. I carry their powers with me. If that wasn't enough, Uriel put the Flaming Sword inside of me so that the fallen wouldn't get it. I died centuries ago, and this is my second go-around."

Luna's eyes were wide. "I feel like maybe the cliff versions aren't good enough."

"Well," Remy said, "that"—*clap*.

I grabbed her hands before she could keep going. "I think what Remy is saying right now is I'm not in a great mental state, so at this current moment, I can't go into details on how eccentric I am." I gave Luna a small smile so that I wasn't being a complete bitch. "I haven't learned how to master all my powers yet, but I can say that the usage of the Flaming Sword is coming as easily to me as breathing. On my first night here, Uriel visited me. Since then, I've dream walked to seven archangels on a plane in heaven."

Luna was almost drooling. Finally, she closed her mouth. "Flaming Sword. Reincarnation. Archangels. Dream walking. I'm done. Done." She flopped dramatically on the bed while mumbling things under her breath.

Trev said, "Why didn't you say anything about the archangels?"

I could feel Remy pulling her hands out of my grasp, so I tightened my hold. I had no clue what was up with her and her aggressive clapping.

"Why would I tell you?" I asked.

"Good point," Ezra said.

"Like I was saying," I continued. "He told me that I could transfer some of the power that the sword held." Looking at Luna, I said, "You now have some of that power inside of you. That is how you killed the wendigo."

Luna started erratically rambling off questions, and I could tell that Remy was dying to clap again. When Luna stopped speaking, the brothers began asking me questions.

"Here is what I care about right now; another archangel, Sandalphon, has asked me not to kill the wendigos. There is nothing we can do about the one that Luna fought off her, but from here on out, we need to heed his advice."

"How many archangels have you talked with?" Trev asked in dismay.

Ignoring him, I said, "I cannot get a mark on me. That means that we have to work quickly because, as soon as the headmistress figures out that I'm more than I'm pretending to be, she will try to lock me down here."

Remy rolled her blue eyes. "Can I make an amendment to your plan? We should have killed her first thing, but that was a mistake." I agreed. "I say we just kill her now. We run the Empowered Academy until we can figure out a situation for the wendigos. Then we focus on how to turn the commander back to the hot-ass man he is."

"That's not actually a bad plan," I murmured. "Now tell me two things. How did you return so fast, and what did you find out?"

She shined her nails on her shirt. "So, in ghost form, I can travel the ley lines. It is super cool and, not to brag, but I can travel anywhere in the blink of an eye. Paris? Japan? Alaska? Yeah, and all in the same hour. What? I know, super awe-inspiring, right?"

I tried to return her smile. "That is cool. Now, what did you find out about Finn?"

Her happiness evaporated. "My intel, and by that I mean the Rocks, think that the headmistress sent the wendigos out to where the commander was with his small group of fifty, including the Rocks, to show the commander that the headmistress has a weapon—the wendigos. However, no one from the Academy of Seraph actually saw her or her guards. Their best guess is that she waited on the mountainside, close enough to control the wendigos still, but far enough that the commander wouldn't be a threat to her. They believe that the commander was meant to be harmed."

I took a deep breath.

"The Rocks said that they also believe the headmistress is now aware of what you are capable of."

"Me?" I swiveled my gaze to Trev.

He put both hands up. "I swear to you that, other than my brother, I haven't told a soul about who I thought you could possibly be. Luna knew you were our saving grace, but I didn't tell her why. But if I had put together the pieces, I'm sure that someone else could have."

"Two of the Academy of Seraph's people didn't make it back," Remy said. "They think one of them knew and told."

"How many people know about me?" I asked more calmly than I felt.

Ezra pushed off the door. "They brought them in while Luna was to be the sacrificed. I just heard that they put them in the dungeons. I'll go and see if that has anything to do with Gabriella. Luna, why don't you come with me?"

Luna hugged me. "Thank you for saving my life. You have given me this gift, and I promise that I will not let you down." Though I didn't need her words because of my gut, I appreciated them just the same.

We watched them both sneak out of my room, and then I asked, "And when the wendigos came to fight the fifty from the Academy of Seraph, what happened?" I knew without asking what had happened, but I wanted Remy to say it.

"The commander's scout saw them from a distance. The only good thing about the wendigos is that they aren't faster than the commander, who met them head-on. The first wendigo he grabbed turned the commander into one of them. He then fought every single wendigo by himself. All thirty of them."

I swiped a tear from my cheek. Finn had to become something horrible in order to beat them. If I had returned with Remy in the very beginning, I would have been there with him. I could have defeated the wendigos, and Finn would be okay right now.

Remy pointed a finger in my face. "Nope, we're not doing that. We were led down this path for a reason. And just because it got a little bumpy doesn't mean we are giving up."

I nodded. She was right. We had to stay the course now.

"Also," she said, "he knew what he was doing when he decided to save all those people. He is not lost to you." She nodded vehemently. "My plan is the best. Let's kill the headmistress and redecorate the school in her absence."

"Bloodthirsty," Trev said, "but I like it."

She winced. "Sorry, sweet cheeks, I'm in a noncommitted relationship with your brother."

Trev laughed before a buzzing sounded from his pocket. He pulled out a small cell phone and frowned before he said, "I have to go meet up with Ezra and Luna. I'll be right back."

"Everything okay?" I asked. "Well, are things no worse than they were five minutes ago?"

"I don't know, but as soon as I do, I'll tell you."

After he left, I curled up in the bed with Remy beside me.

"You know," she said, "we have to go on the offense on this."

I nodded. "When Uriel came to me, he suggested I bestow the power of the Flaming Sword to six others."

"If we are preparing for battle, don't you think you should get on that?"

"Yeah," I mumbled. "I'm just so tired."

"I know you are. Take a quick cat nap. There's nothing we can do with all the guards surrounding the headmistress. Soon, though, she'll go off to her room to find sleep, and then we will strike."

Remy was savage. Savage was just what I needed. I also needed a replay of what had happened to Finn. My powers were swirling inside of me. I would not dream walk. I would search for the past.

I fell asleep with Remy playing with my hair.

fourteen

I WASN'T DREAM WALKING; I was tapping into
Haniel's gift while sleeping. The gift gave me what I
wanted to see the most—Finn in the forest with numerous
other blessed. The Rocks were flanking his sides, looking
menacing. Finn was scanning over the eerily quiet forest
with his green eyes, and I was shocked to see Mrs. Fields
crouched behind a tree with a book in her hands, quietly
talking about war plans and strategy to a young blood
beside her. She didn't look happy to be in the forest. I
wondered if Finn had made her come.

Hannah came up to the trio of men. Her reddish-orange
hair was up in a messy bun, and there was a smudge of
dirt on her face, covering half her freckles. She crossed
her long pale arms over her chest and cleared her throat.
"Commander, I appreciate you letting me come today."

Finn sighed. "I didn't let you come, Hannah. You snuck out with the seniors."

She looked like she was about to pass out, and Finn wasn't even shouting. "Um … yeah, I guess I did do that. Regardless, I wanted to know if you needed me to be a decoy of some sort? Maybe instead of waiting here, I could travel by myself to the Empowered Academy. I could say that I wanted to join their ranks; try to get close to Gabriella to see how she's faring."

He shook his head. "We already have Remy on the inside. We don't know what we are dealing with yet."

"But, Commander— "

"No, Hannah, the answer is no." When her bottom lip began to tremble, he sighed. "Listen, I know that you are worried about Gabriella, but she is strong. She has a plan and told us to wait here, so we will wait here. You and I both know that, if she wants the headmistress of the Empowered Academy dead, then the woman doesn't stand a chance. There must be a good reason Gabriella has asked us to wait, so we wait. Your friend, Remy, can't be killed. Not twice. She is just as safe as Gabriella. You are not. You should be back behind the walls of the Academy of Seraph, but due to your disobedience, you are here. Don't make me have someone escort you back."

Her blue eyes filled with unshed tears, but she nodded as she walked back toward a group of students hidden behind a few oak trees.

"She just misses her friend. Wants to help," Dan said.

Finn clenched his jaw. "We are all feeling a little useless right now, but one thing I don't need is someone inexperienced going behind enemy lines and getting themselves killed. Gabriella loves Hannah; it would hurt her."

Richard nodded. "What do you think the headmistress has up her sleeve? I smell no demons."

"I don't know."

"Rest assured, boss, the Flaming Sword can kill any demon, any angel," Dan comforted. "She will be fine."

Mrs. Fields cut her eyes to the trio of men. She then raised her eyebrows for a second before she turned back to her book.

Dan had just let it slip that I had the Flaming Sword inside of me.

Before Finn could say something, a noise echoed from the steep hill before them. Then a young boy shouted, "Sir, Sir! There are creatures heading our way!"

"Stay here," he commanded Dan and Richard as he stretched his massive black wings from his back. "Keep them quiet," he ordered before he jumped in the air and began to soar above the tree lines. He took in the sight of the wendigos making their way down the steep climb. Their bodies were massive as they made their way up from fifty below. They made no sign of trying to be quiet, and why would they? They would track their prey, and there was nothing anyone could do about it.

With a swoop, he changed directions, heading back

toward the forest. He landed so hard the ground vibrated. The look on his face was determination and anger.

"What is it, boss?" Dan asked.

"She has created wendigos."

Richard said enough curse words that a sailor would have blushed. "How the hell did she do that?"

Finn shook his head. "It doesn't matter. We can't kill them. Both of you are to run the academy until further notice."

Dan shook his head. "No, boss."

Finn ignored the big man as he once again took to the sky. So focused on the wendigos, he never saw the tall, redheaded girl, who had been eavesdropping, making her way through the forest and toward the mountain.

He landed in front of the first wendigo. His beautiful wings were outstretched as a sexy smirk, the one that I loved more than anything, stretched across his face. He looked like he was about to entertain guests, not sacrifice himself.

The wendigo came to a screeching halt before he lunged for the commander. The other wendigos stopped on the trail, watching as Finn reached out and grabbed the first wendigo by his throat.

The dream faded, and I thanked the Lord for that. I didn't want to see Finn turned into a wendigo.

My turmoil turned into peace as Haniel's gift receded and I began to dream walk.

There, Finn stood, at the edge of a lake. The water was

almost transparent. It was beautiful, but I couldn't take my eyes off the man in front of me.

A blanket appeared on the grass that led up to the water.

Without turning around, he asked, "Did you have a bad dream?"

"Yeah." I sniffled. "Finn, I—"

"Come sit for a while?" He turned then.

I nodded as I bit back tears. He knew what I had dreamed of, and he didn't want to talk about it. I thought it was purely for unselfish reasons. He knew it had upset me, and he didn't want to see me upset.

Trying to act as if my heart wasn't breaking, I walked toward the blanket where we sat side by side for half an hour, holding hands, watching the sun glisten on the water and listening to the birds chirp without ever saying a word.

Finally breaking the silence, I said, "In this new form, you can create where you want to meet?"

"No, I've always been able to do that. But this"—he nodded at the lake—"is better than where I currently am." He raised our held hands to his lips and gently kissed my hand. "I'm sorry."

I turned my head slightly so he wouldn't see the tears forming in my eyes. "For what? Saving your people? Our friends? Never apologize for that. Besides, if I had come to you when you sent Remy for me, you wouldn't be a wendigo right now ... so this is all my fault."

He grabbed my chin, forcing me to turn my head and look at him. "Gabriella, the Flaming Sword is a great gift, but there is no way you could have fought off all those wendigos with that power only. Who knows what would have happened if they would have jumped you? Maybe even you can be turned into one of them. There are too many unknowns. Besides, because I'm fully blessed, or maybe it's because I'm Lucifer's son and have dark magic already inside of me, whatever the reasoning, I'm extremely powerful. I have the advantage of killing the wendigos in a fourth of a second. My claws slash through their necks, and in the next moment, they are nothing but a pool of black oil. I am sure you will learn to wield the Flaming Sword faster, but until then, there would have been casualties. Could you live with that? What if one of those people were Hannah? This was the only way."

"I would never sacrifice you so that others could live, though."

A sexy smirk crossed his face as he bent his head toward mine. "I missed you," he said as he laid me down on the plaid blanket. Then he shifted so he was laying me.

Looking up at him almost took my breath away. Every inch of him looked like he came from the bloodlines of a fallen angel. He was studying me just as intensely as I gazed upon him.

I suddenly felt shy with the thoughts running through my head. My wants were almost embarrassing.

He brushed my hair away from my face. "Don't ever be shy or embarrassed with me, Maka. Not ever."

My lips unconsciously parted slightly as he moved his

lips closer to mine. For a moment, we focused on nothing but the kiss. Then I felt the soft brush of his warm hand as he trailed it down my rib cage so slowly that I thought I would melt into the blanket. As he slid over me, he still managed to somehow keep his weight from crushing me.

I ran a hand up and down his chest, feeling the concrete wall of muscles. And, as he trailed his lips down their steady path of my destruction, I turned my head to give him a better angle for my neck that he was currently making a trail down. That was when I noticed his biceps flexing and moving. That sight alone made me moan.

He chuckled as he stopped at the base of my throat. "Thoughts, Maka. Whatever you do, don't control them."

"What are you doing to me?" I asked.

He kissed the space above my collarbone. "I want you to burn for me. When you're not with me, I want you to remember how my breath against your neck made you pant like you're doing right now. With every thought of me, I want your heartbeat to accelerate." He placed a kiss over my heart, and I thought I was going to lose my mind. I threaded my fingers into his hair, and he raised his head. Green jewels stared at me with raw lust. "And Maka, I want you to remember that I don't do anything half-assed."

I felt the dream start to waver, and he immediately stopped his onslaught of kisses. His eyes pierced mine, filled with need, sadness, and lust.

"You have to go?" His voice was raspy.

Frustrated, I grabbed ahold of him as if I had any say in

the matter. "No."

The dream started collapsing, and I shouted, "No!" as I was jolted awake.

fifteen

"WAKE UP," CAME FROM A feminine voice. She shook me harder.

"No," I said. I wanted to stay with Finn.

"Come on, Gabriella. This is important."

I cracked my eyes open, but I wasn't a happy camper. "Luna? Man, you have the worst timing ever." I was mad, angry, and frustrated as I sat up in bed. That was when I noticed Remy was standing behind her with a worried look. "What is it?" I asked.

She bit her bottom lip. "I have horrible news."

I clenched the comforter. "I was asleep for what, twenty minutes? How could things possibly get worse?"

"Trust me, honey bunny," Remy said, "things can always get worse."

My stomach dropped.

Luna pushed Remy forward. "You tell her."

Remy sat down next to me. "Good news first. The headmistress doesn't know that we know that she knows that you are more than you seem. The bad news is she knows that you are the Flaming Sword."

"What do you mean?" I asked at the same time that my door busted open and Trev came in with his brother right after him.

"I need you to listen," Trev said. "Do you remember Ms. Fields from the Academy of Seraph?"

Of course I did. The woman hated me. She had made my life miserable during her Archangels 101 class, and she was the one I saw in Finn's memory, looking hateful as she crouched behind a massive oak tree. Miserable and hateful.

"Yes."

"She was one of the ones who were out in the forest with the commander."

"Okay?"

I swear that boy rolled his eyes. "She overheard the commander, Dan, and Richard talking to Hannah about you. It was implied that you could handle yourself here, but she couldn't. When the wendigos began their trek down the mountainside, Mrs. Fields began to panic. She knew that none of them would survive, and then the Academy of Seraph would be left vulnerable. She went up the backside of the mountain to negotiate with the headmistress."

"I'll kill that old bat!" I seethed.

"Too late," Ezra said. "Someone beat you to the punch about fifteen minutes ago, and I'm betting it was the headmistress who killed her. She probably got all the information out of her that she needed then exterminated her."

"Good," I said.

Remy shrugged at Trev. "Seems as if we are all a little bloodthirsty."

I stood up and paced in front of the small group. "The headmistress knows exactly what I carry inside of me. She also knows that she can't attack me. My best guess is she is going to try to figure out a way to make me a puppet for herself."

"If she can get you marked, you won't be able to leave," Ezra pointed out.

Trev shook his head. "Something isn't adding up. She knows that Gabriella can easily kill her, but she can't kill Gabriella. How will she get her to use the sword under her command?"

"Yeah," said Luna. "Why isn't she up here right now?"

"She's stalling," Remy supplied.

"For what?" I stopped pacing as a thought struck me. "She is going to use someone who I love to get me to do her bidding. I bet she's out there right now, searching for Finn, and once she realizes that's a dead end, it will turn to others."

"Yeah, like me," Remy said. "Because we know that I come right after the commander. I mean, I *should* come

129

first, but I get it. He's hot, and you both have that whole loved you in another lifetime thing going. So, second place it is."

I narrowed my eyes. "She doesn't know about you, though."

"Who else would she go after?" Ezra asked.

"Hannah," Remy and I both said together.

Luna tensed. "What does she look like?"

"Like a freaking giraffe," Remy answered. "Tall, skinny, and she has bright orangish-red hair. You literally cannot miss her."

Luna closed her eyes. "Oh no."

"What?" I asked.

Ezra shared a look with Luna, who cleared her throat. "We went to check the dungeons earlier. They wouldn't let us down to level one, the level that you were on."

Ezra nodded. "But one of the guards said it was a girl who wanted amnesty. The guards didn't give us a description, but they did say that she was pretty roughed up. We were all so focused on getting more information about Mrs. Fields that we didn't pay the newcomer any thought."

"I want her out of that cell *now*." My voice was stern.

Remy let out a few colorful cuss words. "Here is what we are *not* going to do. We are not going to act like this is the movies where we come up with some half-assed plan, then don't execute it. Or worse, have the opportunity to put a bullet in the bad guy's head, but at the last minute, we shoot him in the leg instead. Then said bad guy comes back for vengeance and murders the whole family, including the family pet. Nope. Not happening."

"I agree," I said. "Let's go for the jugular."

My gut told me what needed to be done, and I was going to listen to it.

I stood up, faced Trev, and then laid a hand on his chest.

"What are you doing?" he asked.

"I am still mad at you, but I get why you did what you did, and desperate times call for desperate measures. I would like to give you some of the power from the Flaming Sword. Is that okay?"

He gripped my hand. "I promise that I won't let you down again."

I nodded as I closed my eyes and concentrated. Power flowed through me and into him. Unlike when I pumped it into Luna, I had better control and more confidence. Therefore, it didn't rush from me in one big jolt as much as it felt like it gently flowed from me.

After a minute, he said, "I don't feel any different."

"Trust me; you are." I stepped over to his brother. "You don't know me, and I don't really know you, but my gut is telling me that you will fight for what is right. Will you accept some of this power? You will never be able to release it, and you will forever be tied to this group."

He gave me a sexy smile. "Babe, if you think I'd let my younger brother have something this cool and not want it for myself, you're as crazy as you are beautiful. I'm in."

I closed my eyes just as I heard Remy whisper to Luna,

"Ugh, my fiancé is so amazing right now."

The whole room laughed as my palm warmed on his chest.

"All right, Remy, you ready?"

Her blue eyes widened. "I don't think I can. I mean, I'm … you know … I'm different."

I trusted my gut. It was telling me to transfer some of the Flaming Sword's power to Remy. "You ready to be more different?"

She shrugged as she nervously stepped toward me. "If you think it'll work."

"I do." And it did. I immediately felt my hand heating as I pressed it to her chest.

"I won't let you down either," she said.

"Oh, I know. You'd be too scared to lose that best friend status."

She rolled her eyes. "Like that would ever happen."

"Okay, guys, I need all of you to get me to those dungeons and to Hannah. Once I transfer some of the Flaming Sword's power to her, she won't have to fear the headmistress any longer. Plus, I'll feel better knowing she can take care of herself."

"The moment the headmistress knows where we are heading, all hell will break loose," Trev warned.

"So, let's prepare for battle."

They all nodded.

"And like Remy said, shoot to kill. Let's not play around with this. There is too much at stake. Act quick, and I really do believe the Flaming Sword will protect you."

"I'm going to go hide our sisters," Ezra said. "Then I'll meet the four of you in the dungeons."

Remy went into ghost form, her cold air alerting us that she was still nearby.

As soon as our group turned left away, from Ezra, and went down the hall, that was when we knew we were in trouble. My gut warned me that tonight was about to get even crappier.

sixteen

THERE WERE NO STUDENTS LOITERING in the hallways. In fact, you could have heard a pin drop. Luna flanked one side of me, while Trev on the other. I felt Remy fly past us to go scout ahead. Before we even made it down the first flight of steps, she was back and stopping us in our tracks.

"This is bad," she whispered. "They have Hannah on her knees, in the middle of that creepy room that they call a gymnasium, but looks more like a nightclub for losers. It looks like the headmistress is waiting on you. I tried to touch Hannah to give her some of that voodoo sword magic, but either it didn't work on me when you did it, or you are the only one who can transfer the power of the sword."

I hesitated at the top of the landing. Luna and Trev were both looking at me for guidance when I had none. Slowly,

I started down the stairs. This was about to go horribly wrong. I felt I would be faced with options, and no matter what I chose, someone I cared about would be hurt.

My feet carried me to the first floor, where I pushed the golden doors open and immediately felt many eyes on me.

In the very center of the room was the headmistress. She had changed into military garments—olive cargo pants with a matching vest. Her twenty or so guards behind her were dressed all in black. Behind her, there were at least fifty wendigos banging on their glass cage. I skipped over the wendigos and the scowling faces of the guards. There was only one person who I cared to see.

My eyes landed on Hannah. A rag had been stuffed in her mouth, and her lanky arms were tied behind her. Her bright hair stood up all over the place, her pale skin was marred with bruises, but her pale blue eyes were angry.

My power slithered through me, begging to be released. I was going to kill them all.

The headmistress, as if knowing what I was thinking, gave me a smirk. "It seems that I found something that might interest you."

I said nothing.

"You know, Gabriella, I intended to use you when I first met you; show the commander who was really in charge, lure him close to me, close enough that I wouldn't have to leave my creations"—she hitched a thumb, pointing toward the wendigos in the enclosure behind her—"but far enough that he couldn't kill me. Then I realized that it wasn't the commander who I should be focusing on ... but you."

She moved a guard away from Hannah as she took his spot. Then she placed one of Hannah's curls behind her ear. "Mrs. Fields had some insight on you, Gabriella. I thought the woman was batty. I mean, what archangel would put something as magnificent as the Flaming Sword into a girl who wasn't even fully blessed? It made no sense, but then there was Thalan ... One doesn't just die. Or, at least, a fully blessed doesn't. Not without severe measures."

She tapped her finger on Hannah's back. "Speaking of, I've found a way to kill a fully blessed. I've made a special serum from the feathers of an archangel. I can do a lot with this serum. I can mark the ones here, making sure they obey my commands of not leaving, and I can also take an immortal life. You see, once a fully blessed is injected with the serum, it weakens them. When they are at their weakest point, like your dear friend Hannah, you must strip the wings. Then you have to behead them." She spun Hannah around. "Guess who just came into their immortality?"

She jerked up the back of Hannah's shirt and showed me the scars on her back. Her wounds were barely healed, but the puffy, angry marks that ran deep across her pale flesh could have only been caused by one thing.

Someone had stripped her of her wings.

My anger bubbled inside of me until I saw nothing but red. The ground quaked under my feet as a storm brewed outside. It sounded like a hurricane had hit and even the stone building wouldn't be safe. A tree branch came sailing in through one of the gymnasium windows as the wind howled. For a brief moment, the headmistress looked scared before a guard put a blade at the base of Hannah's neck.

"I thought the wendigos could kill a fully blessed, so either your math is wrong, or I'm confused."

She narrowed her eyes at the dig. "You are correct. There are actually three ways to kill a fully blessed. The Flaming Sword, the serum, and a wendigo. But I've noticed that the wendigos, no matter how much I encourage them, won't kill anyone who is remotely powerful. That is the only time that my creatures defy me. But don't worry, love; the wendigos at my back aren't here to kill you. They are here for a completely different reason."

"What is it that you want?"

The headmistress squinted her black eyes at me. "Oh, was I not being clear? I'm going to turn you into a wendigo. Then you will be at my command."

With a nod of her head, the guard applied more pressure to Hannah's neck, causing a tiny drop of blood to run down her pale, smooth throat.

The golden doors opened behind me, and I heard the approach of many feet, but I didn't dare turn around.

The headmistress smiled. "I figured this friend might not be enough. I want you to be completely swayed to my side of reasoning, so I made sure that I had other options." She nodded to somewhere behind me.

Trev swiveled around then cursed right before his fist

137

connected with the wall. Luna gasped.

I really didn't want to turn around. My gut was telling me that I was going to be devastated with what I saw. My emotions were swirling around me as my power surged trying to protect me the only way it knew how by fueling me with more power. Once I felt my power like the armor that it was then and only then did I find myself pivoting.

There were fifty to sixty children all lined up against the back wall, ages twelve and under, and there wasn't a dry eye amongst them. Each one of them had a guard behind them. There was no way that I could save them all. She knew this, and she obviously knew enough about me to know that I couldn't let them die.

That was the moment that Ezra showed up. He came to a halt as soon as he entered the gymnasium then angled himself behind one of the guards with a question in his eye. Obviously, when he didn't find us in the dungeons, he came to look for us. He didn't know exactly what was going on, but it didn't take a genius to figure out that we were screwed.

When I turned back to face the headmistress, there was a smile upon her face.

"Yes, you could probably kill me, but where would that get you? You can't kill me before your friend and these children die. However ... if you become a wendigo, I will take a blood oath that, not only will I not harm these people, but I will have the mark erased on every student and captive here."

My body zinged with the lie. "You will have the mark removed?"

"Yes."

Lie.

"Do you know how to remove the mark?"

"Of course I do. What kind of question is that."

Lie.

The blade was cut farther into Hannah's neck. If she were human, she would have been in serious trouble. I watched as the crimson droplets hit the ground.

If I did this, then the headmistress would have the greatest weapon of all time—me.

I could feel the energy between Trev, Luna, and even Remy. They were waiting to see what I would do. I could even feel Ezra's eyes from farther behind me. The path that I was heading down was destiny. I could feel it.

With confidence, I said, "I agree."

With a triumphant sneer, the headmistress said to her guards, "If one of them moves the wrong way, take Hannah's head, along with the children's."

Whimpers sounded from behind me, but I refused to look.

"Follow me," the headmistress ordered.

When Luna and Trev started to flank me, she commanded them to stop. They both looked at me with questions in their eyes. I gave them a terse nod as I followed behind the headmistress and toward the glass enclosure. A handful of her guards flanked me as I was pushed to my knees. None of the guards took their eyes from me.

The headmistress didn't even need her guards. As long as Hannah's life, along with the young innocents' lives, were at stake, I would do anything to ensure their safety.

I wasn't sure what a demi who had been blessed by numerous archangels, while also carrying the essence of the Flaming Sword inside of her, would become once I was turned into one of those beasts, but I had a feeling that I wouldn't be as easy to control as the headmistress hoped.

One of the guards talked through his earpiece, telling the other guards to stand by. He let me know that I better comply with the headmistress's wishes without putting up a fight.

"Continue to face the glass and don't move," she ordered.

I shook my head. "No, I'll have the blood oath first. Then we can proceed."

The headmistress chuckled. "Here I was hoping you'd forget about that." She walked over to the wall where the lever was that would release the wendigos. "Truth is … I can't unmark the marked. There is only one person who can do that, and for her to do that, I would have to untie her, and then she would kill me." She gave me a wink. "It's a good thing we have you where we want you." She was telling the truth.

I glared at her as I faced the glass wall. If it were possible that I could actually turn into a wendigo, I would then kill her. At least, this way, I could be with Finn again.

"Release a wendigo," the headmistress ordered one of

her guards. "I have a feeling we will have to drain her of her power."

As the guard did her bidding, the headmistress said, "Once you live in the pit, you will meet Thalan's first creation. She is the only one who can refuse my call, so we have her restrained. Remember that, Gabriella, if you disobey me, I'll have you restrained, and then you'll never get to come out and play." She smiled fondly at the wendigos.

I was giving her my best what-the-hell look. Was she really giving me idle chitchat and warnings right before she turned me into a beast? *Maybe not the right audience, lady.*

My hands shook in nervous anxiety. Sandalphon had told me not to kill the wendigos. Uriel had told me, more or less, to go down the more challenging path. Well, it didn't get more challenging than this. They wouldn't have led me down this road just to see me fail. I had to keep the faith that I was sitting here, facing the glass that would soon release a wendigo, for a reason. Also, Chamuel had told me to trust myself. My gut was telling me that I was right where I needed to be.

There was a steady stream of cries and whimpers coming from the children.

When cold air swirled around me, I told Remy, "It's okay." The headmistress thought I was giving myself a pep talk.

I watched as one, lone wendigo in the front stretched to its full six feet before it slightly slumped over. Its naked body glistened under the lights as it slowly walked toward the now-open glass like it was reveling in anticipation. As it got closer to me, it cocked its head to the side.

"I command only one of you to come out and make Gabriella here into a wendigo. If it doesn't work, then another of you will come out."

When it hesitated, the headmistress commanded louder.

Finally, it began to creep toward me.

I ignored the tightness around my heart and the flood of emotions that were rolling over me. Then, before I could take my next inhale, there were screams, and a huge commotion was coming from the guard's earpiece. Children were running every which way.

The guard closest to me shouted something that sounded like "hold the line" before he said, "Hello? Hello?"

Looking at the headmistress, he told her, "Communication is down."

When another wendigo came out of the glass enclosure, the headmistress looked startled. "What are you doing out? Only one at a time. Get back in there!"

Guards in the very back of the room looked like they were fighting with a sandstorm. A large object was moving so fast that even the fully blessed eye could not track it.

As the storm moved around Hannah, Ezra quickly ran up and rescued her from the middle of the eye of the hurricane then ran for the door. Trev and Luna were ushering kids through the golden doors. The older kids ran for the door without asking for permission, but the younger ones were terrified. I had every faith that Luna and Trev would get them to safety.

As soon as Ezra got Hannah out of the gymnasium, I stood up from my knees.

The wendigo before me had paused, as if it really didn't want to come near me. The headmistress shouted for it to hurry up.

Before it reached me, we all heard through one of the guard's earpieces a frantic shout. "What is this thing? It's killing all of—"

I smiled as the guard's voice trailed off. I wasn't sure what was attacking them, but it wasn't hurting the children. I also knew that the playing field was now different. There were only a few guards left—the ones who had flanked me.

My power flared inside of me. The headmistress didn't know it yet, but these few men, along with herself, were no match for me.

A guard grabbed my elbow, and I spun into him, laying my palm against his chest. He was dead before he hit the ground.

I took a step away from the other two approaching guards while keeping an eye on the headmistress and wendigo. The sandstorm came whirling to a stop beside me, and my mouth dropped open in shock. The biggest wendigo I had ever seen stood beside me with murder in his black eyes.

Both guards looked shocked as they turned to face the wendigo.

"How did this one escape?" The headmistress shouted.

One of the guards, who was crowding closer to me, shook his head. "I don't know, ma'am."

"Now!" the headmistress shouted.

The smaller wendigo had edged closer to me while I was transfixed with the menacing-looking one. Then, as the wendigo reached for me, a chain of events began to unfold.

I grabbed the wendigo while I chanted silently to myself, "Don't kill, don't kill, don't kill." Unfortunately, the wendigo hit the floor. The good news was it didn't turn into a pool of black oil, so maybe I hadn't failed Sandalphon after all. Then again, the thing wasn't moving.

The headmistress's eyes widened, and then she pointed at the huge wendigo. "Change her into a wendigo *now*."

I could have sworn the wendigo smiled before he bared his teeth at her.

She took two steps back before she turned and made a run for the door. The guards weren't so lucky. The menacing-looking wendigo was upon them before they could flee after the headmistress, tearing the remaining two guards to shreds.

I bit back bile as I looked at their remains. A grizzly bear would have done less damage.

When the wendigo stood upright with blood dripping down his black talons, tears flooded my vision as the strings around my heart tightened.

The wendigo's chest heaved until it saw the trail marks left by my agony, then it roared.

As it started to flee, I screamed, "Finn, no! Stop!"

It was too late. He was gone.

The strings around my heart loosened, and I knew that, with his unnatural speed, Finn was already miles and miles away.

I didn't know how long I stood there, crying, but eventually, Remy was shaking me.

"Snap out of it, chicka."

Then she shouted, "Ezra, make sure the glass doors are shut tight. That's all we need right now is a party of wendigos."

As Luna walked back into the room, she pulled her pink hair up in a high ponytail and scrunched her nose in disgust over the mutilated bodies. "Guys, does anyone want to explain what just happened to me? Did I really just witness a vigilante sandstorm?"

I shook my head. "It was a wendigo."

Ezra ran a hand over his chiseled jaw. "That whirlwind out there was no ordinary wendigo."

"No," Trev said, "it was a wendigo that had been fully blessed."

Ezra's eyes searched mine. "And perhaps it had a touch of the devil in it."

"Not it," I said. "He will never be just an it."

The moment Luna caught up, she said, "Oh shit."

Remy rubbed my back. "You can say that again."

A gurgling sound came from behind me, causing me to whirl around. The moment I saw who made that noise,

I laughed as Luna and Remy cheered. Even the brothers were smiling from ear to ear. Things were looking up. Everything would be okay. I just had to track down Finn.

seventeen

WE HELPED THE NAKED BOY to his feet, and then Luna took off her sweatshirt and handed it to him. He tied it around his waist like a loincloth.

He had shaggy, reddish-brown hair that hung to his shoulders. Dark brown eyes were narrowed as he looked around at his surroundings.

I stepped forward. "Hi, I'm Gabriella. You probably need a minute. Do you want to sit down?"

He groaned. "I feel like I've been on a year-long acid trip. My whole body hurts." He looked at his hands, turning them over and over. "I can't believe I'm me again." He lifted his brown eyes to search our gazes. "How did this happen? I thought I would be stuck like that forever."

Remy clapped me on the back. "Our girl here is *amazing*! One little touch from her and … *poof*, you were standing

in all your naked glory, right here in front of us to ogle."

I gave the boy a nod. "I wish I could stay and chat but I need to go check on our friend Hannah. I'll be back." I started to leave when Trev shook his head.

"When we dropped her off in your room, she asked to be left alone. She probably just needs a half hour to process. She's been through a lot."

She was one of my best friends, so I didn't think that I would count when she said she wanted to be alone.

Remy touched my arm. "Let's give her half an hour, okay? And then we will break down the door if she refuses to let us in."

I nodded. "Okay."

I needed to keep busy, or I would fall to pieces myself. The boy and our victory was all but forgotten as I started to think about Finn.

Trev cleared his throat. "Gabriella, I know your instinct is to go after Finn, but I think, if you chase after him, he will run or, worse, go into hiding. He is unbelievably powerful in this new form, and it must scare him."

Remy nodded. "He doesn't want to hurt you, babe."

"The bond is obviously still there," Ezra added. "He can sense when you need him, like tonight. My suggestion is we lay a trap for him, and he will come to you."

I wanted Finn now, but what they said made sense. "What kind of trap?"

"The marked still need to be free," said Trev. "Just trying to figure out how to do that will be dangerous. Plus, now that we know you can change the wendigos back to their original self, there will be moments when you are naturally scared. The commander will sense your fear."

I thought back to what the headmistress had said. "And I know exactly which wendigo marked your people—the one that is tied up."

"Without the headmistress, though," Luna piped in, "we won't be able to control the wendigos." She looked around the room. "She wouldn't happen to be part of this carnage, would she?"

I shook my head. "Afraid not. She escaped while her guards were being torn to shreds. I should have gone after her, but I'm pretty sure I was in shock from seeing Finn in that from. He ripped into the guards like a wild beast." We all did our best not to look at the mess that was puddled on the ground. The newcomer couldn't help himself, though, and started to gag. We all pretended not to hear him. I was a sympathy gagger, and that was *all* I needed right now.

I focused on the glass cage that held three wendigos. Earlier, Ezra had hit a button, closing the glass doors. Walking over to the lever I started experimenting on how the controls worked. I flipped the lever downward, and watched as more wendigos came crawling up from the floor. They stood around looking at us and tapping the glass before one by one they grew bored and started to go back to the pit below. When there were only three left again, I flipped the lever. I was scared that more would come up. I could have waited to see if the last three would go back to their pit, but it was a gamble.

"Well," Remy said, "we now know which lever releases the beasts." She winked at the naked boy. "No offense."

"It's Porter, and none taken."

"Cute. So, anyway, we release the wendigos by popping that lever and hitting the big red button next to it, have our girl here restore their humanity, find the one tied down, work that magic on her and, bada bing, bada boom, everyone is released from this hellhole. Then we beat Gabriella until she fears for her life, luring back the hotness. We change him back to said hotness, track down the headmistress, and kill that bitch. The end." She took a curtsey.

We all just stared at her until she said, "Oh, I'm sorry. Was that plan too easy for all of you?"

Trev shook his head. "We can't just release all of the wendigos at the same time. If they overpower us and make it out of here, we will have literally released hell on earth."

"Also," Ezra said, "we aren't sure yet if we can stop them, too, or just Gabriella."

Remy rolled her eyes. "She shared with us her power, um ... so I don't know about you lame-os, but I'll be able to stop some damn wendigos."

"They do have a valid point, though," I told her. "We're going to have to let them up one at a time." I looked over at the pale, tired-looking boy. "Porter, how many wendigos are down there?"

He shrugged. "Too many to count. A thousand maybe?"

I pinched the bridge of my nose. Why could nothing in life ever be easy?

Everyone was quiet for a few moments.

"Okay," I said. "We need to turn the wendigos back to their demi or fully blessed status. Like the brothers said, if they accidentally escape, we're screwed. This should be two birds, one stone. When we come across the original, she will lift the mark on the academy's people."

"Luna, can you release everyone from their cells and get them into suitable rooms? And take Porter with you."

"Of course." She took off running.

"Ezra, get ahead of her and gather all students, staff, and if there are any guards left, and tell them that—"

"There's a new sheriff in town!" Remy shouted. "And if they don't like it, the power of the Flaming Sword shall strike them down." She shook her fists in the sky while laughing in a deep voice.

I grabbed one of her hands and brought it back down. "The extra power is making you a little cray-cray."

"Nope. Don't try to give me an excuse. I was born this way."

I shook my head. "Ezra do you think that the headmistress has another way to get to the wendigos?" My gut was saying no but I still needed to ask the question.

"I do not think so," he said. "Someone saw her flying from the academy. With most of her guard's dead I don't think she'll return. At least not tonight."

My intuition was telling me that he was correct. "Ezra,

please tell them that the headmistress is no longer in charge, and once we free the people of their mark, I will be absolving this academy. And if they have an issue with it, they can come see me."

He saluted me. "My pleasure."

"Yasss, baby, yasss," Remy purred.

Lord, give me patience.

I turned to Trev, who was chuckling. "Please don't encourage her." Then I clapped my hands together and said, "Let's start releasing these wendigos one at a time. I don't feel tired after changing Porter back, but I'd like to test my limits."

"And maybe you can train us, too," Remy suggested.

I nodded, though I wasn't entirely sure how. Using the power of the Flaming Sword felt natural, like breathing.

Trev clapped his hands. "Then, we begin." He locked the golden doors that led into the room.

I watched as one wendigo came forward and bashed his hand over and over against the glass wall.

"Aggressive little booger," Remy commented.

"You ready?" Trev shouted.

I nodded as I faced the glass wall and waited. Trev went to the wall and pushed the button that opened the glass enclosure. Once one wendigo came into the room, he immediately pushed the button again, closing the doors.

"Here it comes!" Trev shouted.

"Remy, go block the door just in case it makes it past me."

"On it," she said as Trev came to stand beside me.

The massive wendigo strutted into the room as it tilted its head back and roared loud enough to cause me to jump. I let it walk to me. I wasn't meeting it halfway.

"Trev, you need to step back," I said, but before he could the wendigo backhanded him in the wall that was at least fifteen feet to my right. I wouldn't be able to outfight it. It had too much power and strength. The wendigo threw a fast right punch and I barely had time to duck under the wendigo's arms. As I came up behind him, I knew I had to act quick so I shoved his back with my palm as I silently commanded him to turn back into its original form.

The wendigo stumbled forward before it hit the ground instantly.

Remy's eyebrows crashed together. "Dude, did you do something wrong?"

"No. It takes a minute."

The three of us sat and watched the wendigo turn back into the fully blessed or the darken that it used to be. Maybe once the headmistress if fully out of the picture all of the darken will realize that they can choose a different path. The wendigo started gaining color to its pale skin. The veins no longer were visible as it began to morph. The body began to shrink as the dark magic left the wendigo. If I would have blinked I would have missed the black nails disappearing and the body hair coming back. When female body parts started taking shape the boys turned their back. It was truly an amazing transformation.

While the naked female got her bearings, Trev went to score some blankets for the other naked people we were about to have. When he came back, we were done explaining to Terra what had just happened. Then I did the remaining two.

Trev let up an additional two that I changed back before I started feeling tired. It could have been the lack of sleep or that I was literally draining myself. I couldn't find it in me to stop, though.

Remy had checked on Hannah, who was dead asleep. If I couldn't comfort her, I might as well be productive. Besides, the more blessed I brought back, the more chances we had of freeing everyone, and I needed Finn to come back to me. Maybe if he felt me draining myself, he would come back.

When there was a knock on the door, I didn't bother turning to see who Remy let in as Trev released another and another.

Finally, Luna came up beside me. "Let one of us give it a try."

"No, I got this."

"Of course you do," Remy said. "We are just going to give you a little break."

I looked around the room. Ezra was now back to leaning up against the golden doors. The last wendigo that I had touched was lying in a corner with a blanket thrown over its body, waiting for it to return to normal. I had stopped taking the time to wait until the blessed came back to us.

I wasn't debriefing them anymore either. However, I heard soft voices behind me and knew that someone was cluing them in. It wasn't going to hurt me to let someone else take over and help.

I rubbed my chest. Finn wasn't near.

"Okay," I said, "listen up. I'm learning as I go, too, but this is what I know about using the Flaming Sword. Whatever I think happens, happens. When I was under attack at the Academy of Seraph, I thought to myself that I had to survive. Hannah had to survive. Those thoughts alone stopped Zack, because he died. When I wanted to give each of you the gift of the Flaming Sword, I did so with just a thought. When I touch these wendigos, I want them to turn back. I don't want them to die. Think about it, and it will happen."

They all nodded.

Luna hung her head. Without meaning to I plucked grief from her thoughts.

"What's going on, Luna?"

"That wendigo that I killed, he or she was just like all the ones you've turned back so far. They were just innocent blessed, trapped in a form that they didn't ask for. I murdered someone."

Her thoughts were ramming into me—pain, grief, shame. I had to build walls around my mind to escape from them.

I squatted in front of her. "Luna, that was not your fault. Did you know you had the power to kill a wendigo?"

She shook her head.

"Did I tell you what you were capable of?"

Again, she shook her head.

"Then, if we are going to blame someone, blame me."

She jerked her blue eyes to mine. "I can't blame you, but I can see what you're doing. Thank you for that."

"Luna, all of us are new to this. We are going to make mistakes. I decided to save you, and because of that, a blessed died. I will have to live with that, and when I have time to grieve, I will, for Hannah and for that blessed. Just know that this was not your fault."

Ezra cleared his throat as I stood up. "I'll go first."

"No, the hell you won't," Remy said. "I've been watching her for almost two hours using this party trick, and I want me some of that. My turn." She jumped up and ran toward the glass. Bouncing from foot to foot, she said, "Okay, I'm ready."

I went to stand by the doors next to Ezra just in case the thing made it past my friend. I was beginning to feel emotionally and physically drained but I needed to remain steadfast. Every minute that went by I realized more and more how many people were truly counting on me. I stood up taller as my eyelids grew heavy. I watched as Remy popped her neck and threw out a couple of right hooks to the thin air.

I called out, "Remy they are extremely strong. You can't hesitate. You have to be quick about it."

"Yeah, yeah," she said. "I got it."

What happened next would have been comical if I hadn't been so tired.

The doors opened, but the wendigo just stood there, staring at Remy. She whistled and patted her legs like she was calling to a dog. It tilted his head at her. Then she started lecturing it on what a proper wendigo would do. When the wendigo still didn't move, she whined, "I think mine's broken. Maybe you should have had this one, Ezra."

With her guard down, the wendigo then tackled her to the floor.

We all stood there in shock as they rolled around, and Remy cussed better than any sailor on any ship on the sea. The wendigo grabbed a handful of Remy's hair and pulled.

"Remy!" I shouted. "Use your power."

"Hello! I'm trying."

The wendigo screeched as it pulled more of her hair.

"Oh em gee, are you from Jersey?"

Trev walked closer to the rolling pair. "Need help?"

Remy slapped the wendigo, causing it to shriek again. "No, I don't need help." She put her hand against the wendigo's chest. After a few seconds, the wendigo stopped fighting and passed out. Remy then crawled on her hands and knees toward Luna, who had tears streaming down her face because she was laughing so hard.

"I'm a ghost, but in this form, shit hurts. And you"—she pointed at Luna—"if you think that was so easy, why don't you go next?"

Luna winked at her as she walked toward the glass doors.

Her ponytail bobbed and swayed with every energetic step forward.

I was trying not to tap my foot impatiently. Even if we did twenty conversions a day, it would still take us at least fifty days, according to the Porter's estimate that there are a thousand wendigos. My gut was telling me that we didn't have fifty days. We didn't have fifteen. I felt this need deep down in my soul to rush. It could be because I needed Finn to be okay, but I couldn't shake this feeling that something big and nasty was headed our way and we were running out of time.

Luna handled her wendigo much better, but as soon as the wendigo was down for the count, so was she, as her knees buckled.

Trev helped her back to her feet. "You okay?"

"No, I feel like I'm about to be sick." She looked at me with embarrassment. "Maybe I'll slowly be able to build up how many I can do in a day."

I gave her a nod. "One is one more than we had five minutes ago."

Trev went next. He was able to do four before his legs became shaky. Ezra pulled in another four.

"I want to go and check on Hannah again to see if she is up yet," Remy announced.

"You just checked on her," I said.

"Just let me do me. I can float in and out. That way, if she's still asleep, I won't wake her."

"If she's still asleep, that is the best thing for her," Ezra told her. "Remember we heal faster when we are asleep."

Remy nodded. "I won't wake her if she is. I'll be back in an instant."

Remy came back within minutes, reporting that Hannah was still in a deep sleep.

With nothing else to do, I got back to my feet as everyone rested. The sooner we freed the wendigos, the sooner the people marked were free.

I turned three more wendigos when my vision started to go a little black. I convinced myself that I could do one more. Just one more, and then I would rest. I convinced Trev that I was good, even though the look on his face said he didn't believe me. The moment the wendigo was released into the room, my legs began to shake under me. I didn't think the others in the room had any more left to give. I had convinced them that I could do this, and if I failed them and let this creature get past me to their loved ones, they would never forgive me.

Time stood still as I began to panic.

"Trev, push it back behind the glass! She can't!" Ezra shouted.

But it was too late. The wendigo saw an opening for freedom and was going to take it.

The strings around my heart tightened. As I began to sway on my feet, there was a sound of collective gasps. I put my hands out to the wendigo that was barreling toward me when a light so bright and pure hit it square in the chest.

It fell to its knees before face-planting into the cheap flooring.

Out of the corner of my eyes, I caught a flash of crimson. My wings were out.

The sounds of awe faded into shouts of concern as I felt hands grabbing me. Before my eyes unconsciously closed, I realized I was cradled against the chest of a wendigo, and not just any wendigo, but the one who owned my heart.

eighteen

I WOKE UP OUTSIDE OF the Empowered Academy. I was leaning against a bank of soil that had formed around a giant rock. The bank was cutting off the chill of the night wind, with a terrifying-looking wendigo crouched in front of me.

I reached up to cup his jaw. "I know you are still in there."

The moment that the wendigo knew I was awake, he stood to his full height.

I tried to sit up, but everything started to spin, so I dropped my head against the dirt of the bank, telling him, "Finn, listen to me. I can change you back. Not now because I'm depleted, but I can. I promise."

The beast before me clenched its fists and dropped its head back, howling at the night sky. The sound that he

made felt like it would crush my soul if he didn't stop.

I tried to stand, but the movement had me passing out into a blissful sleep.

I searched for him in my dreams, but it was of no use. What I did find was just as heartbreaking.

I met Hannah in her dreams. She was on her knees, the slab of cement ice-cold as I walked across it. She had hundreds of black feathers in front of her, and she was raking them toward her while tears streamed down her face. When she noticed me, she let out a sob.

"Gabriella, I thought I was dreaming."

I nodded. "You are, my friend. Remember how I can dream walk?" I reminded her gently as I knelt beside her. "I think I recognized your need to talk to someone."

She looked at my torn shirt. "Did your wings come out?"

As she dreamed of what was left of her wings, I found it hard to answer in truth. "How are you feeling?"

She fell to the side and pulled as many feathers as she could into her lap. "My birthday was the day after you disappeared."

I reached over and grabbed her hand. "And I wasn't there for that. I'm so sorry."

"It's not your fault that you got kidnapped. When I came into my powers fully, it was nothing like what you experienced. My symptoms were so light that I was able to hide it from everybody. Plus, I was really worried about you."

I scooted so close to her that I was almost in her lap with the feathers. Sometimes, people weren't looking for you to solve their problems. They just wanted someone to listen. Being what she needed at the moment, I encouraged her with a nod.

She sniffled. "So, I ignorantly thought that I could help against whatever the evil headmistress threw our way. I thought she had demons. I didn't even know that wendigos existed, except for in old folklore."

"What happened when you saw the wendigos attack?"

She laughed without mirth. "They didn't. The commander attacked first. When I saw him turn into one of those things, I panicked. The commander is the commander, you know?" I did know exactly what she was saying. "He has this kind of power that radiates off of him. It's magnetic and, at the same time, it's terrifying. I couldn't think of a possible thing that could take him down. Honestly, I still wouldn't believe it if I hadn't seen it firsthand. Then he turned savage."

She hiccupped. "Gabriella, my psychic abilities are so much stronger than anyone predicted, and I swear it's because you helped me. I read the commander's thoughts. Except … it was no longer the commander. It was a beast, and all he could think about was the raging hunger that demanded him to kill."

"Go on," I said, holding back my tears. Hannah needed me to be strong.

"While the commander destroyed the wendigos that were coming down the hill, I hid behind them, in a crevice between two rocks. Everyone was running back to the Academy of Seraph … except for one person."

"Mrs. Fields?"

"Yeah. Man, I hate her. I knew what she was up to. I caught onto her thoughts so easily. She was going to betray you.

"I couldn't immediately chase after her, because I would have had to give up my safe spot, and I was terrified that the commander would turn on me next. I waited until he finished with the wendigos. He made this guttural sound, and then he ran through the woods as blood dripped from his fangs.

"I was just about to crawl out of my hiding spot when a guard came down the hill. There was no sign of the wendigos; instead, there was just black liquid everywhere. He bent down and put two fingers in the crude oil and smelled. I plucked his thoughts from him. He had no clue what the liquid was. When he stuck his tongue to the black oil that coated his fingers, I almost gagged and blew my cover. Then he felt fear. Fear that he had to go back up the mountain where the headmistress and more guards were and tell them that, not only was the commander and his people missing, but so were the wendigos."

She smiled at me then. "I got to use my wings."

"You did?"

She nodded. "I taught myself how to fly. I made it to the academy, but not in time. Mrs. Fields beat me there, and what's worse is she saw me come in. She told the headmistress all about me and how we were friends. Little did she realize that, after she gave the headmistress everything she needed then told her how she could bait you, the headmistress no longer needed her.

"Guards held my arms and forced me to watch as Mrs. Fields got injected. Then they forced her wings out of her back and ripped them from her." She rocked back and forth. "I can still hear her screams. Then, after her head was taken from her shoulders, the headmistress turned to me and said, 'You're next.' I fought so hard, but it was no use." She started crying so intensely that her body shook.

I wrapped her in my arms and swayed her gently. "Hannah, I'm so sorry. If I could make this right, I would do it a heartbeat." I felt so useless.

Hannah pulled back from me. "Someone is trying to wake me."

I smiled. "It's Remy. She knows that sleeping is the best thing for you, but she's worried. Plus, she just saw a wendigo take me. She's probably freaked out."

"What?" Hannah gasped out.

I waved it off. "Nothing. Tell her I'll be back soon."

I watched as Hannah disappeared. Her feathers disintegrated when she left the dream.

I began to wander for what felt like hours, praying and

hoping that wendigos needed sleep. I was starting to give up when I found him.

He sat on a dock in the middle of a lake, his legs draped over the edge, his feet submerged in the dark water. He had on a pair of shorts, and that was it. His perfect chest and abs glistened in the fading sun.

My eyes trailed over his carved biceps and forearms as he ran a hand through his wet hair. I studied him. To say that he was handsome would be like calling a Michelangelo painting a drawing, instead of a work of art. He was almost overwhelming to look at.

I walked to the edge of the water, noticing that not only was I still barefoot, but I was in a red bathing suit. Gone was my torn dress.

His eyes scorched a trail over me, leaving everywhere they landed feeling burned.

I ran a hand over my body. "Did you do this?"

He gave me a smirk. "You coming in or not?"

I waded waist-deep into the lake. Chill bumps popped out over my body.

"How come I couldn't find you?"

He looked off into the distance. "It takes the wendigo a while to calm down and rest. Here, I have control. With him, there is no control. He worries me."

I shook my head. "Not me. It's still you trapped inside. I never felt like he would harm me." I was trying desperately to reassure him. However, the look on his face told me that he was far from convinced.

I swam out to the dock, and he extended a tan arm to me then hauled me up beside him. I pushed my dark, wet hair back then kicked my feet through the water as we sat in silence and watched the last of the sun fade from the sky.

He scanned the calm water as he finally said, "When I don't come to you like this, I need you to not think of me as Finn. I want you to think of me as only a wendigo." He flashed his eyes to mine. "This means something to me. Promise me." He truly was terrified that he would lose control.

"I promise that I will try my hardest to think of you as a wendigo."

He nodded. "Not Finn, but a wendigo."

Reaching out, I grabbed his hand. "Finn, I can turn you back. I was exhausted earlier, but I know, when we wake up, I'll be able to."

"How?"

"It's the Flaming Sword inside of me. It allows me to free the blessed trapped from their wendigo form."

His green eyes looked distant. "Maybe I'm meant to stay like this."

My mouth dropped open. "What? Why would you even say that?" I squeezed his hand. "I don't think you're listening. I can fix this. I can help you change back."

"You are not the only one who the angels visit."

I watched as he slid off the dock and into the lake, dropping even his head under the water.

Groaning, I followed him into the lake and swam

toward the bank, only stopping when I saw him pop up from the water. He stood there, waist deep, waiting for me to come to him.

I ignored the water droplets that ran down my face. "Finn, who came to see you? Which archangel?"

"Maka, listen to me. A long time ago, I didn't protect you. I failed you. This time around, I will do anything to make sure that I don't lose you again. Even if it means I need to stay a monster, I'll do it."

My feet sunk into the mushy bottom of the lake, and I did my best not to cringe as wet mud slid between my toes. "Finn, you don't need to stay a wendigo. That's what I am trying to tell you. I can destroy the wendigos or turn them back to what they once were with just a thought. Who would you need to protect me from?"

He trailed his hand down my cheek. "Even you, Maka, are not infallible. But with me in your corner, you might have a chance for what lies ahead."

I was getting angry. "And what exactly is that?"

"If I tell you, then you will choose me."

I crossed my arms over my wet bathing suit. "So, there is an option where I don't choose you?"

That damn sexy smile lit up his face. Then he raked his teeth over his bottom lip, and I sighed, causing him to laugh.

I waved a hand between us, trying to air out whatever magic spell he had me under. "Wait a second. You're being all allusive. I need facts, and then I'll make the choice that needs to be made."

He grabbed my hips and pulled me toward him. "The night grows more chilly. You need to wake up."

I rolled my eyes. "I'm immortal. I don't think I'm going to catch a cold."

His hand trailed my ribcage. "Did you know that you can be hurt while dream walking?"

I guessed I had never really thought of it. I felt lust ninety-nine percent of the time when visiting Finn in my dreams, so it made sense that I could feel other things, such as pain, as well.

I felt the deep rumble of laughter coming from Finn. He rolled over so he was looking up at me. "Only ninety-nine percent? I'm doing something terribly wrong then."

I smiled before I grabbed his head pulling it down to mine laying a gentle kiss on his lips. When I pulled back, his face had lost all joy, and worry coated his words. "You can be hurt. Any dream you walk to, even if it's manifested like this lake we're in, it could still harm you. If you had hit your head on the dock, you could take on water and drown in your sleep. The issue with searching for me is that, not only is it unsafe in the dream, but you found me. What if someone startled me awake before I could be entirely cognitive? You could have a wendigo in your dream. That's just dangerous. You wouldn't get this Finn. You would get the wendigo."

I bit my lip as I digested his words. I understood his concern but this was the only time that I got to see him.

I would be on my guard but I wouldn't stop wanting to see him.

He said, "Let me have one kiss before you need to go."

"Go? I'm not going anywhere. You just don't want to talk to me about me changing you back." I didn't get to say anything more before he crashed his lips against mine and rubbed his wet body against mine. I thought I was going to have a mini-stroke as a fire ignited in my bloodstream. Then he slanted his mouth over mine, and there was nothing tender or soft about this kiss. It was ravishing. It was as if … as if … he was getting his fill of me.

I pushed his chest as I reared my head back. "Finn, you better tell me that was not a goodbye kiss."

He ran his thumb across my bottom lip. "Of course not. Haven't you been listening? I don't aim to lose you again, Maka."

I poked a finger at his chest and winced—damn rock-hard body. "So, you don't plan on staying a wendigo? You are going to let me use the sword to free you?"

He smiled down at me. "Did I say that?"

"That's the problem! You're talking in circles. I'm so confused."

He dropped his lips back to mine again. This time, he was slower and more gentle, teasing me with his tongue.

I felt myself leaving the dream world once again, but not before I heard him say, "And that is how I'll kiss you hello when all of this is over." He was pushing me out of the dream and forcing me to wake.

My eyes popped open, and I looked around me, finding I was still lying up against the bank in the cold. The only difference was there was no looming wendigo. Finn was gone entirely.

nineteen

THE WHOLE WALK BACK TO the Empowered Academy, I raged as I talked to myself like any true, going-around-the-bend psychotic would. Sometimes, I even answered myself. Like who doesn't have time to cry over the hottest boy in the land? Me that's who. And why is that? Because I'm super busy kicking ass and taking names. I could have used my wings to take me back, but the truth was that I needed a moment to think and calm down.

I stomped through the lavender fields, not even enjoying their smell or their beauty. My mood had the flowers reaching to me to try to comfort me, but I was not in the right frame of mind. The blooms almost looked like they had enlarged as I walked by. That was new. Since before I was eighteen trees and plants would respond to my moods but it was clear that my powers that were given to me were

growing daily. Once I broke through the field and toward the forest, I was ready for murder.

How could he not let me fix him? Did he *want* to be a damn wendigo? Of course he did. I didn't understand his thought process, but I knew he felt that, by him staying a wendigo, he was somehow protecting me. I wondered which archangel dropped in to talk with Finn. If I could just get him to myself for more than thirty minutes, we could actually have a real conversation.

The leaves on the trees began to rattle as I continued to fume. I took a deep breath, trying to calm myself. All I needed right now was all the trees being uprooted.

Turns out that my gut and intuition was also like a GPS of sorts. I knew exactly where I was. I made the climb up the side of the mountain. A few bats flew down close to me, and I shooed them away. I couldn't even find happiness in the fact that my night vision was fantastic. I could see pebbles on the trail from ten feet away. I should be ecstatic, but I just felt grumpy as hell.

I saw a young man on top of the roof of the academy. He shouted to someone behind him, "She's back. Tell them she's back."

I stormed into the academy, seeing a few students still milling around, even as late as it was. They smiled and nodded at me. I just grunted as I passed them.

I had only made it up two flights of stairs when Remy almost tackled me down the steps.

"You're okay!" She hugged me so tightly to her I thought

my ribs would break.

"Pissed, but okay. We will talk about the whys later. I'm emotionally drained, and I need to check on Hannah."

"She's in the shower." She grabbed my hand like she was afraid I had forgotten how to climb steps. "We need to have a meeting, pronto."

We ran into a tired-looking Luna at the top of the steps. She scanned me from head to toe then hugged me. "Hey, girl. I was worried about you."

I waved off her words. "No need to worry."

Remy nodded. "Could you please tell Trev and my *ex*-fiancé that we will be in Gabriella's room? They need to meet us there."

She gave Remy a wink. "You got it, firecracker."

Remy ushered me to my room. My anger was starting to fade a little, and I realized how tired I was.

She pushed me onto the bed. "Sit. You look like you are about to fall over." She tilted her head toward the closed bathroom door. "Hannah is in the shower. When she gets out, don't talk to her about you know"—she dropped her voice to a whisper—"her wings. She is going to be fine. She just needs some love, that's all."

I didn't tell her that I had already spoken to Hannah. Instead, I just nodded. I did agree that we should let Hannah come to us when she wanted to talk. Hannah had been through a hell that none of the rest of us could understand.

I kicked off my shoes and crawled under the covers,

clothes and all. "So, did I hear correctly? Ex-fiancé?"

Her blue eyes flashed. "Yep. It's so over."

A smile lit up my face. "And why's that?"

"Well, when the wendigo came in and grabbed you—that was the commander, wasn't it?"

I nodded.

"So, when the commander took you out with a blurry speed that none of us could track, I might have gone a tad crazy. I screamed for Ezra, who was the closest to the door, to go after you, and he said, 'Meh. She'll be fine. It's not like he's going to kill his soulmate.'" She nodded, her short black hair swinging about her chin. "*Meh*, he said. Talking about the potential harm that could fall upon my bestie and the boy said, *meh*! No, girl. Right then and there, I broke things off. I can't be with someone like that. I'll have to cancel the wedding registry, but a girl must do what a girl must do."

I had no words. Nothing.

My head hit the back of the headboard as I heard the shower turn off. Hannah was going to be okay. She was definitely going to have to work through some things, but she was alive. And as soon as I saw Finn, I would light him up like the Fourth of July, with or without his permission. He was beyond ridiculous.

"So," Remy said, "red wings, huh?"

I grimaced. "Yeah, I'm assuming everyone saw that?"

"Yeah. Well, everyone except for Hannah. Which, considering the circumstances, I don't think it's appropriate to talk—"

The bathroom door swung open. "You both do realize that I'm still fully blessed, even without my wings, correct?"

I scooted up in the bed a little as I studied Hannah. She had a soft, white towel around her. It was super short, because she was runway model tall. Her hair appeared darker, due to it being wet, and her eyes were puffy; evidence that she had been crying pretty hard in the shower.

"How are you feeling?" I asked.

She lifted one dainty shoulder. "That guy, the one who's Trev's brother, healed me. I feel no more pain, which is a blessing. That was the worst pain I've ever felt."

There was a knock on the door, and I shouted, "Who is it?"

"Luna."

"Come in."

Luna came in, carrying a stack of clothes. "Hey, girls. I thought that you could share some of these items. I'm sure Gabriella wants out of that dress that looks like a pillowcase, and I knew Hannah would need some after her shower." She laid them down on the bed. Then she sat next to the pile, her gaze running over Hannah.

"I know that you don't know me, but I'm hoping that'll change. I have spent my whole life with only friends who were boys. I'm pretty sure I'll say things that are crude and inappropriate from time to time, but hopefully, all of you will forgive me?"

Remy scrunched up her little nose. "Um ... crude and

inappropriate is kind of a staple for this group."

Luna laughed. "How are you feeling, Hannah?"

Hannah sighed. She was probably going to get that question a lot.

She walked over to the pile and grabbed a shirt and a pair of sweatpants that would probably be too short for her. She slid them on under her towel then put the shirt on as she shimmied the towel down. We waited as she wrapped the towel around her still dripping hair. Then she walked to the other side of the bed and pulled back the covers, crawling in beside me.

Looking at Luna, she finally said, "Obviously, there are scars on me that won't heal, even though I was immortal—am immortal. They are bad, but that's not really what has my emotions all over the place. There is a huge sense of loss. I didn't have a ton of time to even get used to my wings. I only got to take to the sky once. Maybe that's what is really bothering me. I can feel that part of me that I know is missing, like how I imagine an amputee would feel phantom limb pain. It feels as if they are still there, even though I know that they're not."

Remy was drying her face. Luna had grabbed Hannah's leg that was under the comforter and was rubbing it. I grabbed one of her hands while searching for the right words.

"Hannah, I can't give you back your wings. I don't know of anyone who can. Nothing I say or do will help you grieve less over their loss, but I can give you a gift."

"It's true," Remy said as she moved the clothes to a chair in the room and sat next to Luna. "Hannah, I felt the same way as you. Not quite, but almost. Someone killed me, took my life, and then I ceased to exist. It was a bitter pill to swallow. Everyone forgot about me. After a few weeks, I didn't even hear my name being murmured in the hallways. They had moved on with their lives, a life that I didn't have anymore.

"When Gabriella came to the school and could actually see me, I was so damn happy. Then she gave me an extra gift." She gave Hannah a watery smile. "She gave me you. And now look at me. I'm able to use my ghost form as a power. I can go invisible when I want to, and I am just as immortal as the fully blessed. Maybe more so. Then I received another gift."

Hannah gave her a questioning look, but before she could answer, Luna said, "Gabriella decided to give me a gift, as well. I was seconds away from either dying or becoming a wendigo, and Gabriella gave me the power of the Flaming Sword. I'm not good at using it," she said sheepishly, "but I think I'll get better."

Hannah unwrapped the towel from her hair. "What do you mean, she gave you the Flaming Sword?"

I shook my head. "I didn't give it to her. I poured some of its essence into her. She, along with Remy, now carry it around with them."

She narrowed her pale eyes. "They can do what you can do?"

Remy scoffed. "We weren't touched by eight archangels, but we can wield the Flaming Sword. We can kill wendigos with a touch of our hands. Of course, we choose not to."

"You aren't killing them?" Hannah asked.

"Nope," I said. "We can use the sword to turn them back to their original state."

"You're kidding!" she gasped.

"She's not," Luna said. "And here is a really cool part … We're not certain, but we don't think that we can be killed. I mean, if we can, it would be really hard."

"We should probably test that theory out on Ezra," Remy suggested.

"We can," I said. "Or, at least, an archangel told me that if I exhausted all my powers, I could die."

"Bummer," Remy said.

I grabbed Hannah's hand. "I'd like to give you this gift, too. It won't bring back your wings, but it will give you a purpose. We will rely on you. If you choose to accept this, you will be forever tied to us in an unbreakable sisterhood."

Hannah's bottom lip trembled. "I think I would like that very much."

All of us were smiling as I touched my palm to Hannah's chest. She closed her eyes, and a small smile lit up her face.

Remy clapped. "This is the best girls' night that I never wanted."

We all laughed.

"So," Remy said, "I hate to bring up darker times after this kumbaya moment, but what happened with the commander?"

I groaned. "The man is infuriating. Honestly, in his wendigo form, I barely spent time with him. It was when I passed out and dream walked that I saw him. I told him that I could change him back to fully blessed. He didn't act shocked, but he did argue that he should *stay* a wendigo."

"What?" Remy screeched. "Like, for good?"

"No," I said. "I don't think he plans on staying like that forever, but one of the archangels came to visit him, and they explained that perhaps it would be better off. He thinks he will lose me if he can't protect me, and other than the Flaming Sword, nothing can take down a wendigo, other than a wendigo. So, the more I think about it, he must think that a wendigo is going to harm me."

Luna took down her ponytail then ran a hand through her pink hair. "The fact is that everyone who we've turned back from wendigo to blessed remembers their time as a wendigo, but it seems that it's a bit foggy. Even the powerful ones describe it like they are strapped in the passenger seat, taking a joyride, as they watch their life being managed by someone else."

Remy nodded. "For Finn to still be in control is an amazing feat. He never once tried to hurt you, and from what we understand, once a blessed becomes a wendigo, they belong to their creator, which is the headmistress. Technically, she should be able to control him."

"When he thought I was hurt, he carried me away from the academy. He watched over me until I healed enough to walk back." I ran a hand over my chest. "I can feel him. He's close, but not close enough."

Remy shook her head. "What a sad group we are. Luna, you're new, but I'm sure you have some baggage, right?"

She nodded. "The headmistress forced my parents to do some recon for her. To make sure they did their job she put me and my little brother in a cell. When they died we lost all hope of freedom. Then to make matters worse I survived. My brother did not."

We all winced.

When she saw how depressed we all became she said, "Then to make matters worse I became like a little sister to the brothers. They have been bossing me around since I was fifteen."

"That is good enough. I'm sure that it has provided you with great psychological damage," Remy said. "Hannah, my little giraffe, is a mess, Gabriella's love life is in the gutters of hell right now, and I had to call off a very high profile marriage to a boy who I found I could no longer love."

"Whaaat?" Hannah began.

Luna and I shook our heads, trying to warn her, but she ignored us both.

Remy smiled. "So glad you asked, friend."

We all groaned as she began her version of two star-crossed lovers spiel. When she got to the part about how their love was as rare as unicorn babies born in Spain, I feigned sleep. I noticed that Luna was curled like a kitten in a little ball at the end of the bed. At some point, me faking sleep turned into the real thing. I had expelled a ton of energy today, and my body was exhausted. I rested easy, knowing that Ezra had set up a few guards to alert us if the headmistress was headed this way. We wouldn't get much sleep because the brothers would eventually come and wake us, and Finn was somewhere nearby. My wendigo wouldn't let anything bad happen to me, even if he had to remain a wendigo to assure it, which I was still mad over.

As dreams took over, I prayed to see him, but I couldn't find him, no matter where I searched. However, it did seem that someone else was waiting for me to fall asleep.

twenty

A BEAUTIFUL WOMAN STOOD IN an empty space. There was nothing but darkness surrounding her. She was the only light in the room. Her skin was a light caramel, and her shiny black hair hung to her waist. She looked like a better mixture of Zoe Saldana and the singer Ciara.

She cocked her beautiful face to the side. "I don't know of these people."

She had read my mind. Of course she had. "They are famous people who live on earth."

She looked like she was still confused, but she nodded anyway. "Do you remember me?"

I did. "I've seen you in my dreams before."

She looked a little saddened by this. "But you don't remember me from your first life?"

I wanted to lie just to ease the pain in which I saw on her

face, but I said, "No, I'm sorry."

"It's okay," Jophiel said. "I was hoping to visit with you soon."

I looked around in the darkness. This was the first time I had ever dream walked or been summoned through my dreams where the place felt utterly isolated and void of anything. There was no warmth or light anywhere to be seen.

"Where are we?"

Her beautiful face looked so sad that my heart hurt. "Unfortunately, this is my home. When your mother— when *we*—lost you all those years ago, some of my brothers and sisters were sent back to heaven by the blade that Azrael used to carry. We wept for those seven, even though, ironically, getting back to heaven had been our plan all along. Of course, none of us wanted to accomplish our goal by the end of the Flaming Sword. That would mean, when we returned to heaven, we could never leave. The issue with that is we had all fallen in love." She gave me a beautiful smile. "With you. In you, we saw our hopes and dreams of what we wanted this world to become. After you were born, we all wanted to stay on earth; see how you fared. It's bittersweet how things work out like that." She let her chin drop to her chest for a second. "I miss my brothers and sisters."

I didn't know what to say, so I nodded.

"The day of your wedding changed all of us somehow. The remainder of us scattered and, unfortunately, I am stuck in this place."

Now I understood why the beautiful creature before me looked so broken. "Tell me how I can help."

A smile lit her face. "I was hoping you would ask that. There is something you need to know about your love. The longer Finn stays a wendigo, the harder it will be to turn him back to the blessed that he is. Every day, he will lose a little piece of himself. The more powerful the blessed is, the harder it is to convert them back. I'm well-aware of what you are trying to do for the blessed who are trapped as wendigos, but you need to realize your limitations. Stop before you are too exhausted. What if you pushed yourself to the brink, and then the next one that comes up from the portal is extremely powerful? The Flaming Sword could combust inside of you, killing you."

"So, I need to rest and then force Finn to turn back before I lose him?"

She shook her head. "No. He needs to stay a wendigo for the time being."

I was so confused. "But you just said that the longer he waits, the harder it'll be to change him back."

"Yes, but there is a monster waiting in the plane that is extremely powerful. One that will attack you full force in wendigo form, and you will kill yourself trying to stop it."

"You're talking about the original wendigo?"

"Yes, and killing the original wendigo will have repercussions."

I didn't plan on killing any wendigos. "I will turn the original back to its true form."

"I need your Finn there to make sure that you don't exhaust your powers." I nodded. "I also need you to understand that the power a fully blessed holds is completely different from a wendigo. They are both powerful and strong, but in different ways."

"It was you who visited with Finn?"

She nodded.

"If I can get Finn back, I can pour some of the power from the sword into him. Uriel visited with me, and he said that there would be seven who carried it. Finn is the missing link."

She gave me a sad smile. "I'm afraid that he must remain a wendigo for the time being. It is the only way to save you from the original. Even with everyone you have given the Flaming Sword gift rallying with you, you are still no match. She is the original, the first wendigo ever created. She is hundreds of years old, and she will tear you apart. Her power will break all of you. You do not stand a chance. Not without a wendigo on your side. The favor I ask of you is do not try to convince Finn to come back to you. Not yet."

I swallowed the lump in my throat. "It's not fair. I feel like there is always some huge obstacle in our way."

"A love like yours will prevail, even against death. In fact, it has already done so."

I dashed a tear away. "So, he has to stay a wendigo for the time being?"

She nodded.

"At least I'll still get to dream walk with him until I can change him back."

She gave me a beautiful smile. "The more you use the power of the Flaming Sword, the better at it you and your friends will get. I know you are on a time crunch, but remember to stop before you get exhausted."

"Exhaustion is just a word. I've been nothing but tired here recently."

"This is a different type of exhaustion. Your vision will cloud, and you will see black dots. More than likely, your nose will bleed because, at this point, you're hurting internally, and Chamuel's power will be screaming for you to stop. If you don't listen to your instincts, you will die."

"Thank you for the warning."

"One more thing, Gabriella. Thalan used dark magic to give the headmistress the power she needs to call the wendigos. They all belong to her. As long as she lives, the wendigos can and will be used against you. Even the wendigo who loves you, and the longer he lives as a wendigo, the harder it will be to disobey her commands. Never forget that."

Her hair shimmered as she turned.

"You're leaving?" I asked.

"Yes, my love. This exhausted me. Hopefully, I'll be able to call you back soon, though. Take care, niece."

I exited the sad void just as quickly as I had come into it. I woke up feeling drained. All four of us were crammed on the tiny bed.

I quietly pulled back the covers and went to the window where it overlooked the backside of the academy, where the forest and lavender fields lay. I placed my forehead up against the cold glass plane, wondering what Finn was doing right now. Would we ever get out of this mess? Could we ever just be normal?

twenty-one

THE FOUR OF US GOT a couple of hours of sleep that night before the brothers, Trev and Ezra, came to get us. It was time to have a meeting, a game plan of sorts. My room was overcrowded, so we headed toward the school library, which was a joke in comparison to the Academy of Seraph's library. This room was more of a make-out session for students. We each had to go down the rows and break couples apart before we had them exit. Hannah's skin was as bright as a flame by the time we ushered the last grabby couple out of the library. Then we grabbed a table in front of the doors to make sure no one entered without us noticing.

After we all took a seat, we waited for someone to start the conversation. I cleared my throat.

"So, we all got a few hours of sleep. It's not ideal, but it

is good enough for us to continue with the releasing of the blessed from their wendigo bodies. I don't think any of us need to fully exhaust ourselves today."

Trev nodded. "Agreed. I also think one of us should not use the Flaming Sword today. We could all rotate on who should or shouldn't use the power. That way, if something bad does happen, one of us will be refreshed."

That was actually a good idea, except I didn't believe I should be a part of the group that sat by and did nothing for the day. Especially since I could convert more wendigos back to their original form, but I kept my mouth shut. I would cross that bridge when I came to it. Besides, the way Trev looked at everyone except for me, I had a feeling he knew that I wouldn't agree to those terms either.

Remy said, "It's been quiet for almost twelve hours. The headmistress needs the wendigos."

I nodded. "She's not that powerful without her creations." If she had been, she wouldn't have looked at me with fear in her eyes. "It's just a matter of time before she comes back to try to claim them."

"We need to set up a guard in the gymnasium," Ezra said. "Maybe a couple of us."

"Are any of us powerful enough to stop the headmistress without Gabriella?" Luna asked.

"I believe so," I answered.

Trev ran a hand through his hair. "But I don't know if any of us are strong enough to hold back an army of wendigos."

I thought about Jophiel's message to me in the dream. Any of us could be killed. I needed to stop acting so hasty when it came to the lives of the people sitting at this table. Finn decided to remain a wendigo for the time being. I needed to focus on the job I was born to do and make sure no one I cared about died from my poor decisions. That would be something I couldn't live with.

I gripped the edge of the table. "I received a warning on the limitations of our powers yesterday."

"Another archangel?" Trev asked.

"Yes. If we over-exhaust ourselves to the point of self-destruction, we will get warning signs first, like cloudy vision and nosebleeds."

They all remained quiet as they digested my words.

"Okay, who is on the first watch?"

"I think Remy and I can go on right now?" Trev said.

She gave him a thumbs-up. "I'm good as long as another wendigo doesn't try to play tonsil hockey with me."

"Then Luna and Ezra next shift," Trev continued. "Hannah and Gabriella the next."

I was already shaking my head. "No. Let Hannah pick which group she wants to join, and I'll stay with each group."

Hannah grabbed my hand. "You have to eat and sleep at some point."

I pushed back from the table. "We should have had this meeting in the gymnasium. The headmistress could be attacking now, releasing wendigos."

"Not likely," Ezra said. "I found capable seniors who, considering our circumstances, have leveled up to guards. They would have notified us."

"Are we sure that the pull lever, along with the button, are the only things that will release a wendigo from the container?"

"Ninety-nine percent positive," Trev said.

"Then that's not good enough." I was walking toward the doors. "Hannah, pick a group."

I heard the disagreement and mumbles behind me, but I didn't care. I wouldn't exhaust myself. I could sleep in front of the golden doors, but our main concern right now was not to allow the headmistress to release the horde of wendigos.

Once everything was settled, I said, "I have a few things to do to try to protect these walls. I'll meet all of you in the gymnasium." With that, I pushed through the doors and headed outside. A smile was on my face as the five of them followed behind me like ducks. "What are you guys doing?"

"I don't know about them, but I personally want to know how you are going to protect these walls," Remy said.

I shook my head as I came to a stop in front of the academy doors. "Fine, but please stay back."

Closing my eyes, I let the power coil around me before it lashed out. Wave after wave flowed from me to the woods that surrounded the academy's front and sides. "Come to me," I whispered, though I knew my call traveled down the steep mountain and past the lavender fields. Minutes went by before the first few animals arrived. Within half an hour, the front of the school was packed with rodents, reptiles, and mammals.

Hannah whispered, "It looks like the Garden of Eden."

I looked at all the eyes before me. "I need you all to guard this mountaintop. If anyone tries to come into this area, I need you to stop them."

I extended my arm to an owl. With incredible gentleness, he landed on my arm. "Hello, friend. Please scout for us. Let us know if anyone is heading this way."

In answer, he flew from my arm. His magnificent wings spread beside him as he soared to the sky.

"Do we have food for them?" I asked Ezra, who had come up beside me and was staring in awe at a wolf.

"Most of what they would normally eat is sitting or standing beside them."

"Well, we can't feed them to each other."

He nodded. "Yeah, of course not. I'll find food."

"And leave it out here? When they are hungry, they can come for it."

His eyes swiveled to a large elk. "So strange. I don't know why I'm surprised. Yeah, I'll have them food left out here." He took one last look at the wolf then went back inside.

I smiled at the animals. "Thank you, friends. Please go now and guard the mountaintop."

Little feet hopped off toward the border of the top of the mountain. Others crawled or trotted, but all obeyed.

"So creepy," Remy said.

"If you thought that was creepy, you should probably go inside with Ezra," I said. Then I closed my eyes and reached for that thread that I felt inside of me, the one that allowed me to connect with Remy while she was in her ghost form. A burst of cold air surrounded us.

I opened my eyes and looked at the six figures who were steaming mad at being summoned. When my eyes lit on the last figure, my power surged within me.

"You," I said.

Remy's mouth dropped open. "Is that …?"

"Who?" Hannah shouted. I guessed she couldn't see her, yet Remy could, as she was a ghost, too.

I took two steps closer to the ghost. "I see that you decided not to pass through. The only problem is that you are not welcome here. Not even in death."

Mrs. Fields glared at me. "How dare you summon me? You don't control me, nor do you scare me. What are you going to do? Kill me again?"

Letting my power naturally flow, I watched as Mrs. Fields tried to leave but couldn't. My power had anchored her down to the ground. The more she struggled against my hold, the madder she became.

"Who is it?" Hannah asked again.

Remy sniffed. "It's that old, fat face, Mrs. Fields."

Mrs. Fields glared at her. "You know, Remy, I was there the night you died. It's a shame that you can't remember it. I wonder why. Must have been a gruesome death."

I saw my sassy, strong friend blanch.

"No!" I shouted. "You have done enough damage. I want you to pass on. I have a feeling where you will be going will be of a warmer nature."

She shook her grey head. "No. You can't make me."

I raised an eyebrow. "Really?" Spreading my arms wide, I watched as a brilliant white light pushed out of me and landed on the wild-eyed Mrs. Fields. As soon as the light touched her, she burst into a million different images. It was like looking through a kaleidoscope."

Remy gasped. "Dude, did you just blow her up?"

My arms fell to my sides as the light around me died down. "No. I sent her to hell."

Hannah had tears running down her cheeks as she came up beside me and grabbed my hand. "I wish I could have seen it."

Not letting go of her hand, I pushed the power that the angels had blessed me with toward her. Letting all my walls down, I said, "And why can't you?"

I watched as her eyes grew round, and then she was smiling as tears streamed down her face. "I hated that bitch."

I laughed. "I think we all did."

Luna and Trev were looking at each other with confusion. Remy clued them in.

"Gabriella just sent Mrs. Fields' ghost to hell. And now she has five other ghosts looking at her like they are about to be sick."

Whoops.

I faced the other ghosts with my hands up. "Sorry, guys. There is no need to be afraid of me."

"I can see them now that you're touching me," Hannah said. Then she let go of my hand. "Yep, can still see them."

Luna and Trev shoved her out of the way so they could each hold my hand.

Remy fake-yawned. "My girl isn't a circus attraction, people." She looked at me. "Right, freak?"

I rolled my eyes. Ignoring Luna's and Trev's astonishment, I shook out of their grasps while I talked with the remaining ghosts in front of me. "Do each of you know the headmistress?"

They all nodded, and some added a few choice words.

"I know. She wasn't the best person. I'm very sorry that you all have …" I waved a hand in the air, looking for the appropriate terminology.

"Are sleeping with the fishes, kicked the bucket, bought the farm," Remy supplied.

"Okay, they get it," I said.

Luna said, "At least she isn't clapping."

That was true.

Turning back to the ghosts, I said, "If you want help passing on to the next life, I can help you with that."

There were a few murmurs.

"If you're ready now, you can go, but if you would like to hang out a while here, you can. I would like to ask that you keep a watch out for the headmistress."

A chubby boy said, "She's the one who killed us. I'd like

to stay and look for her."

It seemed that everyone agreed.

"That would be great. And whenever any of you are ready to cross over, find Remy, and she can find me."

The ghosts seemed excited as they took off to find the headmistress.

Remy snorted. "Find Remy? What am I now? The official ghost liaison?"

Remy was talking to Luna and an unfortunate Trev about Demi Moore and Patrick Swayze as Hannah and I went back inside. I was getting stares. Some were intrigued by me, but the vast majority were scared. Their fear permeated the air, and I couldn't help but sigh. There was nothing I could do to reassure them that I wasn't the headmistress 2.0 version. They would just have to wait and see that I meant them no harm. Now, the headmistress was a whole new ballgame. I couldn't wait to cause her harm.

twenty-two

TREV AND REMY MET ME inside the gymnasium. I was already gearing up to convert as many wendigos as I could today.

Turning to Trev, I said, "You talked about them being on a plane that was neither here nor there until they were released into their glass enclosure. Do you think that there is another exit?"

"No, not that I'm aware. But if there was, then that would mean that wendigos could escape, so I doubt it."

I sighed. Again, I didn't like the fact that we weren't a hundred percent sure. "Can she make more wendigos without Thalan?"

He shrugged. "Anything is possible. But if she did find someone as powerful in dark magic as Thalan, they would still have to find the right people to turn into wendigos."

"You mean, like a fully blessed?"

"The rumors are that there was something extraordinary about that first wendigo. There are too many fully blessed just under this roof to be 'very' special, and I guess, if we don't know what that is, we won't know what to look for. It took her hundreds of years to create a wendigo. I doubt that she will be able to just create another so quickly."

Remy said, "It sounds like our best plan of action is to guard these wendigos so that she can't get to them, and when the headmistress comes for them, we kill her."

Trev narrowed his brown eyes in concentration. "I just don't see her coming here by herself. What do you think, Gabriella?"

"That she is too scared to come back here, but she is out of options. She can run, or she can fight. I don't think her pride will let her run for too long. She may have figured out that the sandstorm that rained down havoc on her academy was Finn. It's also a possibility that she will try to find him, command him to do her bidding. Maybe he'll succumb."

Trev and Remy didn't say a word, but they were both digesting my words.

I shrugged. "That's what I would do if I were in her shoes. She can't go up against me, not without the power of her wendigos. The most powerful one of all is outside, roaming around." My gut tightened with fear. If she found Finn, the things she could do with him by her side was cringe-worthy.

"Jophiel came to me in a dream the other night," I said. "She warned me that the struggle of maintaining who Finn once was before he was turned into a wendigo will be harder for him as each day goes by."

Remy bit her lip. "That sucks."

"Yeah."

Trev took a couple of steps away. "I'm going to go make sure we have enough blankets for the blessed we bring over. I'll give you girls a few minutes."

As soon as he was a reasonable distance away, Remy said, "You think she is out scouring for Finn now?"

I nodded. "I do. Why not use the most powerful, especially if he isn't behind enemy lines?"

"Do you think you could dream walk to him and communicate that we need him here? Or at least tell him to go somewhere the damn headmistress couldn't find him?"

"Yeah, if he wasn't dream blocking me."

Remy laughed. "Sorry, that was funny. My mind went in a different direction." She took one look at my face and dropped her grin. "Okay, back to serious mode. All we can do is try to find him through your dreams again tonight."

I nodded. "You're right. We have a full day ahead of us without me borrowing trouble."

"You're just being proactive. But, since there is literally nothing we can do, we might as well focus on the task before us."

My brows crashed together. "Whoa! Remy, when did you become so mature?"

She stumbled back as a hand came up to her chest. Her eyes were widened with fright. "Don't you ever direct those kinds of harsh words at me again. Mature? Why not just knife me where I stand? It would have been less cruel."

We were laughing as she left me to approach the glass enclosure.

"Hey, Remy, I know you don't want to talk about what happened the day that you died, but if or when you're ready, I'm here."

She nodded. "I know. It's not that I don't want to talk about it. I just don't really remember much." Without looking at me, she said, "I actually think I'm blocking my memories. Maybe I wasn't in a place to know what happened before, but I think I'm stronger now."

"I could find out for you, if you want me to."

She shrugged. "Yeah, sure. Just not now. Let's wait until things calm down a bit."

She was still terrified of what she would learn.

"Okay, just let me know when you're ready."

Seeing that we were wrapping up our conversation, Trev yelled out, "If you girls are ready to tango with some wendigos, I'm ready to hit this button."

"Let the good times roll," I said.

It might not have been a rip-roaring good time, but we were accomplishing what we needed to. However, the day dragged on. Remy was able to convert two wendigos back into their blessed form, but she was scared to do a third. Trev transformed an additional six blessed, and my count was ten before we all decided it was time to rotate. On the next shift, I didn't help out until the very end, after Ezra, Hannah, and Luna all took turns. I had officially been on my feet for ten hours when Remy and Trev returned. Someone had made me a makeshift bed in front of the doors. I climbed on the sleeping bag and watched them work from a pallet on the floor. My eyes were closing as Trev brought one more blessed over.

twenty-three

FINN LOOKED EXHAUSTED. HIS JET black hair stood up every which way and, paired with the stubble on his chin, it gave him a savage look. There was no pretty scene before me. No calm, beautiful lake or a blanket laid out. We were in some woods that looked vaguely familiar.

"Why are you looking for me?" His voice was scratchy.

"A better question is: why wouldn't I?"

He ran a hand over his tired face. "Gabriella, this form is extremely hard to control. There is a spell that is so darkly woven in it that I'm having a hard time remembering who I am."

I went over to him, grabbed his hand, and led him to a tree. He put up minor resistance as I dragged him down to the ground beside me. I then rested with my back against the tree and told him, "Lay your head on my lap for a

minute."

He hesitated but did as I asked. I ran my fingers through his hair as I talked.

"Finn, an archangel visited me. She explained that the more powerful a blessed was before being turned into a wendigo, the more they would struggle. I'm proud that you've been able to maintain a part of who you are this long. I understand that you are trying to protect me. I searched for you initially to try to convince you to come back to me, but I come to you tonight because I have to tell you something important. I need to let you know that the headmistress is looking for you."

"What do you mean?"

"She can't get back into the academy. Not without a fight. She knows that she is outnumbered. I don't think she can make more wendigos. Not fast anyway. So, her only option is—"

"Me."

I nodded. "There is a good chance that she hasn't put together the pieces. I can tell you from experience that the wendigos that I've brought over, or witnessed being brought over, haven't had the power you have. All of the ones we have turned back have been demis or fully blessed, ranging in different power levels, but none are close to your range."

A rage like no other came into his eyes. "If she thinks she can use me to fight against you, she has another thing coming."

I loved how protective he was of me, even if it meant that personality trait was what was causing him to be away from me right now.

I ran my hands through his hair. This was what I wanted more of—moments just like this. His head in my lap, looking at me like I was the most priceless thing in the world. It would be nice if we could have moments like this without the wendigos and crazy people, like the headmistress or Camaella, who were always trying to kill us, but I would settle for stolen dreams.

Just thinking of the fallen angel had me wincing.

"Finn, I might have forgotten to tell you something, but in my defense, you've been busy being a wendigo, so really, it's not my fault."

He narrowed his eyes. "What's wrong?"

"Before I was kidnapped, I dream walked to Camaella." I could see he was getting agitated, so I quickly said, "Nothing happened. I mean, when she saw me, she recognized me. She thinks that I just didn't die, but there is a good chance that she'll piece it together."

He squeezed the bridge of his nose. I waited for him to say something, but he just sighed. When he opened his eyes, there was frustration behind them.

"Are you mad at me?"

His brows came together. "No, Maka. I'm pissed that you have so many people coming after you, and I have this urge to hide you away."

I bit my lip. "I can't hide, Finn."

"I know," he said, and then we were both quiet for a few minutes before his green eyes began to twinkle. "Even as a wendigo, do you want to know what hasn't changed?"

"What?"

"The wendigo can still pick up your thoughts when you're agitated or have extreme emotions. When I fight the wendigo, I can even tell what you are thinking."

I smiled down at him. "And you like knowing what I'm thinking?"

He reached up and grabbed the back of my head, pulling me down to him. "I really like how dirty your mind gets when your thoughts stray to things that you would never say out loud. When you think you are going to die if you don't get to touch me, those are thoughts that I want to hear again."

My lips barely met his when he began to convulse on my lap. I watched in horror as his beautiful green eyes turned black.

He grabbed my hand that was still tangled in his hair and roared, "Wake up. Now!" He then sat up in a crouch before he grabbed me and threw me a few feet from him. I landed on my back, sticks and rocks jabbing into me as I rolled onto my feet.

"Now, Gabriella. I need you fully awake *now*!"

I was rooted to the spot, unable to move. I knew I should heed his warning, but I panicked and was unable.

He groaned as the veins in his neck bulged. "She is commanding me to wake. I can't wake in this form, and if

I turn into the wendigo here, in this state, I won't be able to control him. Go, Maka. Please, I'm begging you."

I took a few needed deep breaths as I tried to exit the dream world. It was always so much harder to do so when someone wasn't helping me wake up.

With one hand, he threw energy at me, and that was enough to help me tumble out of the woods where I had found him.

I ran down a black corridor, trying to wake myself up. I couldn't see or hear anything, but I could sense something chasing me. I felt the heat of its breath and the icy touch of its fingers as it didn't capture me but pushed me forward. Then nails ripped into my back, causing me to wake with a scream on my lips.

Trev and Remy were leaning over a blessed lying on the ground with nothing but a blanket covering her. The three of them looked at me in shock. Then Trev and Remy immediately left the girl and ran to me.

With shaky hands, I pushed a lock of brown hair out of my face.

Remy looked me over as she wiped the sweat from my face with the sleeve of her shirt. "Holy balls, what happened?"

I pulled my knees to my chest and rocked.

Trev pushed my hair out of the way. "Why is your back bleeding? It is healing quickly but there is no doubt that there were some deep gashes just moments ago."

"I saw Finn in my dream."

"He attacked you?" he asked in shock.

I shook my head. "No. He transformed into a wendigo in our dream state and chased after me. I'm not sure if he drew blood because he was trying to push me away from him or if it was to help me wake up. Either way, he saved me."

Remy nodded like she had never lost faith in the commander. "Of course he helped you. That's good news."

I looked at both of them. "The bad news is the headmistress found him. He could be on his way here."

Trev cursed, and Remy winced.

All hell was going to break loose, and it was going to be because the boy I loved was going to bring it with him.

twenty-four

WITHIN MINUTES, TREV HAD THE others in the gymnasium, and then I caught everyone up on the dream. Afterward, everyone was lost in their thoughts. I didn't have to tune into Haniel's gift of psychic power to know that they were trying to gauge how screwed we were.

Ezra leaned up against the golden doors. "We have fully blessed seniors here at the academy. I think we should put them on the roof and let them shoot fire arrows at the commander."

I glared at him. He rolled his eyes before he shrugged. "It's not like he can be killed. Also, wendigos hate fire. It might deter him enough that it'll buy us more time."

Remy scoffed. "It's statements like that, along with the over usage of the word *meh*, that got you dumped in the first place, playa."

"I'm confused as to why we care that Finn is coming here," said Hannah.

"Because," Remy started, "if Gabriella is forced between turning Finn back to Finn or killing him as a wendigo, the first is going to win. And, if that happens, there is a good chance she dies, according to an archangel. If she dies, the rest of us are probably toast, too."

Hannah shook her head, reddish-orange curls bobbing every which way. "I didn't know. Why did no one tell me?"

I glared at Remy. If she said one snarky thing like "that's classified, best friend crap right there," I was going to hit her in her best friend face.

She knew exactly what I was thinking, too, as her electric-blue eyes widened before she narrowed them into slits.

"We've all been super busy dealing with stuff, but that's no excuse," I said. "Sorry, Hannah."

Appeased, Hannah nodded.

"So, let me get this straight. Finn is way more powerful than the other wendigos that we've been bringing over to change?" Luna looked pale from the last bout of people she had helped turn back into the blessed. Her cotton candy pink hair was all over the place, and she was in pajamas.

I nodded. "And he grows more powerful every day."

"Great," she commented. "We can't kill him. We can't change him back. There's a potential that he could come here and kill everyone, including the children, or worse, change them into wendigos. We can't leave the building because everyone here is marked, other than Gabriella, Remy, and Hannah, so we are sitting ducks with no options." Her voice had climbed so high she was almost shouting. "None?"

"Whelp," Remy said, "that about sums it up. All we need is an iceberg and Leonardo DiCaprio while some old dudes play the violin, because this ship is taking on water."

"Shit, shit, shit!" Luna started pacing.

"The ghosts won't be any good to us. They can't physically hurt anyone, but the animals can, and the headmistress might be so freaked out that she turns tail and runs. How close exactly does the headmistress have to be from a wendigo to control them?" I asked.

Trev shook his head. "Not sure. I know she has always been within shouting distance when they are released. I think the ones that aren't as powerful can be a good bit farther from her, but she should be in the general vicinity."

"When the commander came in here and tore all of the headmistress's guards to pieces, did she command him to attack you?" Ezra asked.

"Yes."

"And she was close by?"

I nodded. "She was about fifteen feet away at the time, but he was able to disobey her command."

Ezra shared a look with his brother. "Then it is safe to say that she'll need to be close by to make sure he follows her commands. He is too strong."

"If it was any other wendigo, she might be able to be a

safe distance away, but not with this one," Hannah pointed out. "Forget how powerful he is. He loves Gabriella too much. The biggest battle will be the one he wars with himself, and the headmistress knows that."

The chubby ghost, who was going to be one of the watchers for me, came flying into the gymnasium.

Luna made the sign of the cross. "I don't know if I will ever get used to this."

The ghost gave her a wink. "The name is Lane. If you ever decide you want to go for a walk on the wild side, call me."

Poor Luna excused herself. "I'm going to go check on the children; make sure everything is okay."

Ezra and Trev laughed as she left.

"Lane," I said, "did you see the headmistress?"

He nodded. "Yeah, she's traveling with this huge-ass wendigo, but that's not even the crazy part. She is having a hard time controlling him. He went crazy on her. I'm talking bat-shit crazy."

"Do you think that they are heading here?" I asked.

"I don't know where else they would go. When she woke him up, they were in the woods a good distance from the lavender fields."

"Thanks, Lane."

He saluted me. "I'm going to go chill. I'm drained."

We watched him walk through the wall.

"You three ladies are the only ones who can go past the lavender fields," Trev pointed out.

I nodded. "She won't expect us to come to her."

Ezra shook his head. "No, she won't. If you could take her out before she got anywhere close to the wendigos here, that would be for the best. The commander wouldn't be able to infect anyone here either."

"She doesn't know that you have gifted the power of the Flaming Sword to others," Remy said. "Imagine how surprised she'll be when the commander can't infect me or Hannah."

"So, it's settled. We leave now." Remembering how Finn carried me in the air, I said, "I can fly with you, Hannah."

She gave me the first genuine smile I had seen from her since she had arrived at the academy. "I have been waiting to pay that bitch back."

Trev said, "You might need to walk to the lavender fields to try and conserve as much energy. Flying with someone is hard to do."

Hannah's face dropped.

I said, "I would feel Finn if he was nearby. We have time to walk. If you're okay with that."

Remy put a fist in the air. "Yass."

Trev said, "The only way to the academy is through the lavender fields. All roads lead there. The blessed no longer have their wings while they are in the wendigo form, so the commander can't fly to us, and there is no way he can scale the backside of the mountain to get to us. The headmistress won't be too far away from the commander, especially if he is hard to control."

"Okay." I nodded. "Lavender fields it is."

We didn't wait around. All of us were anxious to end the reign of terror that the headmistress had created. And, without her, we wouldn't have to worry about the commander attacking the blessed here at the academy.

Trev and Ezra helped us pack a bag full of food, water, and weapons. Then they each waved us off with a look that was half-encouragement and half-uncertainty, not knowing if we would be able to accomplish the goal we set out to do or not. The truth was that I wasn't entirely sure either.

twenty-five

"MY FEET HURT," REMY COMPLAINED.

I rolled my eyes. "You could go into ghost form and glide your ass there."

Hannah chuckled. "She's just worried we will talk crap about her the moment she leaves."

Remy nodded. "It's true. I don't really want to walk anymore, but I have some serious FOMO going on."

She had a fear of missing out, and I feared that I would strangle her if she didn't quit complaining soon.

She whined again over a rock that was in her shoe. "Guys, did you ever think we would be here? A willowy giraffe, a reluctant student of the blessed, and a ghost, all carrying the Flaming Sword, as we meet up with a boyfriend who is now a wendigo? Will the reunion be a happy one? Nope. It's going to be three levels above being admitted to a

psychiatric ward. But here we are, enjoying our girls' trip, catching up on life. Good times." She stumbled on the path. "Son of a mother trucking back end of a donkey." Stopping us yet again, she pulled her shoe from her foot. A rock came tumbling out. "That's it! I've had it. All good things need to come to an end, too."

Hannah nodded. "Yep, and short goodbyes are the best."

Remy glared at her before she ghosted us. We waited until the cold air around us moved farther along.

"Thank God," I said.

"Heard that!" Remy shouted.

Hannah chuckled.

I threw my arm around her. It was taking us a while to get to the lavender field. The truth was that Remy could have been there in seconds, and I could have used my wings. But, since I had never carried someone before, we were trying to save as much energy as we could and I wanted Hannah to be a part of this. I wanted to make her feel as valuable as she truly is we were walking.

"Thanks for coming with us," I said.

She gripped my fingers that were wrapped around her waist and gave them a gentle squeeze. "I'm fine."

"Never said you weren't. But … if you need to ever talk about—"

"I know."

I followed her lead and dropped the subject.

We were nearing the end of the forest. The area to the right of me looked exactly like where I had earlier dream walked to Finn.

Hannah caught my sigh. "Do *you* want to talk about it?"

I shook my head. "What a pair we are."

"You'll get him back."

"How can you be so certain?"

She lifted a shoulder. "I have never seen two people who were made for each other more than you two. I have a feeling this will just bring you guys closer. True love never dies, my friend. It can morph, it can evolve, but disappear? Never."

It seemed like we all had issues that we wanted to table for the time being. I didn't think that it made us weak. Sometimes, people were like hard boiled eggs—a hard shell that could take a little cracking, but if you kept chipping away, the whole surface pulled off. In my heart, I fully believed that, once Remy saw how good her life was and truly believed it, then and only then would she be ready to talk about the night that she died. And, once Hannah came to terms that she would bring something just as great to this group that we had formed, with or without her wings, she would be willing to talk about what she had gone through when the headmistress had taken them from her. Only time would help her. For me? Well, I wasn't willing to talk about Finn being a wendigo and how afraid I was of losing him until I had him back in my arms.

twenty-six

MY HEART TIGHTENED THE MOMENT we stepped into the lavender fields, and I knew.

Finn was close.

"Remy," I said, "disappear. Your goal is to find the headmistress."

Hannah stayed close beside me as we both scanned the land on the other side of the field. There was nothing.

A frown came upon my face as the strings around my heart loosened. Finn was moving farther away, and I recognized an emotion coming from him that was so unlike him.

Fear.

He was panicking.

I turned in a circle, scanning for him, the headmistress, or both, but there was nothing.

"Hannah," I said, "this is the only way to the Empowered Academy, and wendigos can't fly, but I could swear that Finn is veering off the land to the west of us, farther from the academy. Am I missing something?"

She shook her head, curls bouncing. "No. Suppose the commander was right, and a powerful wendigo can take down even those carrying the Flaming Sword. In that case, the headmistress needs the commander, and she needs to release the wendigos. It's the only way to beat you."

"Us," I corrected. "You carry it now, too."

She gave me a wink. "But she doesn't know that."

I scanned the empty land. Finn was heading down the mountain. There was no doubt about it.

"I'm missing something." I ran a hand over my heart. Finn was moving farther away from the academy, and me, when he should be attacking. Then it hit me.

"Hannah, the Academy of Seraph is to the west. She isn't going to release the wendigos from her academy. She is going to make more! Then she will use that army against us."

Hannah's eyes rounded in fear. "All the students there … None of them will be safe."

We were running through the field when Remy appeared. "Guys, I have terrible news."

"We know," Hannah said. She took another step forward then suddenly grabbed her waist as her face contorted in pain.

Both Remy and I grabbed one of her arms to stabilize her.

Hannah groaned as she took several steps backward. "Shit," she said as she lifted her shirt, looking at her belly.

"What's going on?" I asked.

Opening the band of her borrowed sweatpants, she let another curse out as she showed us her hip. A tiny feather was engraved there.

She looked at both of us with remorse in her eyes. "You need to get ahead of them, and I'm marked; I can't pass this point. You guys go. I'll go back to the Empowered Academy and warn them about the headmistress's plans. Not that we can do much to stop an army of wendigos, but we will do our best." When we both hesitated, she smiled at us. "It's fine." She shooed us before she turned and started to jog back to the academy.

I let my wings out, able to see the fiery red feathers from my peripheral vision. They comforted me but, not for the first time, I felt sorry for Hannah.

"I'll beat you there," Remy said. "So, I'll go ahead and warn Dan and Richard."

I gave her a nod as I took to the sky. Making sure that I didn't fly over Finn or the headmistress, I circled the long way around. I knew that Finn would be able to tell when I got close, but I was praying that he wouldn't be able to communicate that to the headmistress in his wendigo form.

twenty-seven

I LANDED IN THE WOODS of a national park. Now that I knew what to look for, I immediately found the sliver of shimmering air. The only way into the Academy of Seraph was through a magical plane. However, before I could decide whether to go in or not, Remy came tumbling out.

"About time," she said. "I warned Dan and Richard. They have everyone indoors and feel confident that they can keep a wendigo out for at least a couple of hours."

"Good," I said. "It's just you and me against the headmistress and probably one of the most powerful wendigos ever to have lived."

Remy popped her neck. "Homegirl loves a challenge."

"Disappear and keep Finn occupied while I take out the headmistress."

She gave me a say-that-again look.

"That's your only job."

"Only?" she scoffed. "That's cute."

I rolled my eyes. "Seriously? Would you prefer to handle the headmistress?"

"No." Then she narrowed her blue eyes. "Actually, yes. I don't have as good of control over this Flaming Sword business yet, so what if I accidentally fry your lover boy? Or turn Pinocchio into a real boy? No, thanks. That is too much pressure for one girl. I can see it now … The commander throws me around like a rag doll, and as I'm taking punches left and right, because I can't use the Flaming Sword on him, I'll be thinking of why I can't use the power that you gave me, and then I'll accidentally use it! Nope. I'm not doing it. So, that leaves me with the headmistress. Once the headmistress is dead, then she can no longer control the wendigos, right?"

"Yeah, but—"

She pointed a finger at me. "No buts. I'm calling dibs on the headmistress. All I have to do is set her aflame with the mighty power." She frowned at me. "Did you just roll your eyes? Why can't you just let me have my moment?"

"Okay." I threw my hands up. "Have your moment. And what will you do after you strike her with your lightning bolt, Zeus?"

"I will smite her where she stands. She will turn to nothing but ashes—"

"Fully blessed just die. No oil. No ashes."

She narrowed her eyes at me again. "Why do you have

to ruin a good story?"

"Sorry, continue on, Zeus."

"As I was saying, she'll turn to ashes while you lovingly shoo your wendigo away from the magical plane. I'll be doing all the heavy lifting, but I'll be sure to give you credit when we return to the Empowered Academy."

"Aw … That's so sweet of you, psycho. Really appreciate it."

She gave me a wink. "I love it when you call me terms of endearment. So, we know which one we're tackling. This is going to be amaze-balls."

This was a horrible idea, but I felt Finn getting closer, and there was no time to argue.

"Go into ghost form."

She gave me a nod then disappeared right before the headmistress came up a slight incline with a massive wendigo behind her. Finn snarled when he saw me.

The headmistress was still in her cargo pants, but she no longer looked ready for battle. She looked tired and desperate. I was hoping her desperation caused her to make a mistake.

"I'm not letting you into the Academy of Seraph," I said.

"I don't remember asking for your permission," the headmistress snapped. She ran an arm down Finn's new form, causing my belly to tighten. "You see, I have the commander's permission, and that's what counts."

I balled my fists beside me.

"Do not let her close to me and get us in that academy,"

she commanded Finn.

As I guarded the entrance that would take the headmistress into the Academy of Seraph, I silently sent up a prayer that Remy would take care of our problem quickly. As soon as the headmistress no longer had a hold of Finn, ninety percent of our problems would disappear.

The wendigo took slow steps toward me, as if his feet were sludging through mud, and I knew that was Finn's way of fighting the headmistress's commands.

I shook my head. "Finn, stop."

The wendigo balled his fists as he continued toward me. He made a move to grab my arm, but I dodged his talons.

I couldn't kill him, couldn't change him back, and I couldn't let them into the academy. I was in a lousy position. And if Remy didn't hurry the hell up, I would demote her to backseat best friend. No longer would she ride shotgun.

"Remy!" I hissed as Finn swiped his talons at me again, leaving a trail of blood this time.

I stalked closer to the headmistress and away from the magical opening, knowing that Finn would be forced to follow me, thanks to the headmistress's command. That was when I felt long fingers wrap around my hair, pulling me back. I grabbed ahold of the wendigo's hand, but before I could do anything, he jerked me back by my hair then lightly tossed me to the side.

Finn was battling the wendigo for power, and he was winning. A little hair pulling and scratches were nothing to what a wendigo could do to me if they really meant harm.

The headmistress, who just stood there, gloating, all of a sudden let out a gasp. Her eyes widened as she stumbled backward. Then grayish-black wings, that weren't as massive as Finn's but still larger than mine, sprung out as she twirled in a circle. Bending her knees, she shot to the sky, hovering above us about fifteen feet.

I shook my head as I heard Remy say, "Well, shit."

I stood up and ran for the headmistress. I had to end this.

Strong, pale arms tackled me to the ground as the wendigo slid on top of me, pinning me to the ground. He placed his knees on either side of me.

"Kill her!" the headmistress shouted from above us.

The wendigo slowly inched his hands toward my throat.

"I swear to you, Finn, I'll turn you back to your blessed form right now, even if that means my death. So, if you want to stay like this, you better fight her commands."

The wendigo stilled upon me. Ceasing that moment, I grabbed the long, skinny fingers and peeled one back until I heard it crack. The wendigo tilted its head back and roared in pain.

The trees around me began to sway. The largest oak tree, to the right of us, rocked back and forth. When it uprooted, the wind gently blew.

The wendigo registered the incoming tree and jumped up. However, I swiped my leg out and tripped him, causing him to sprawl out in the dirt. I barely had time to roll away before the tree crashed to the ground and pinned the wendigo right where I wanted him. Unfortunately, I didn't miss the tree entirely. A branch from the massive oak struck me in the back with a sickening *crunch* sound. My spine was broken.

I looked up to the sky to see the headmistress in a battle with a ghost, one that she couldn't see, but I clearly could.

Remy was on the headmistress's back. She had one leg thrown over the headmistress's shoulder, and it looked like she was trying to rip a wing from her back. What the hell was she doing?

The headmistress was spiraling, and Remy looked like she was riding a bull. Here I lay, with my spine broken, couldn't even move my damn fingers, and Remy looked like she was at a bachelorette party, waiting to be thrown off a mechanical bull. At least my healing powers would come into effect way before Finn was able to move the tree.

As if he could read my damn mind, the tree began to move.

I wiggled my toes as the damn tree went rolling inch by inch until it was entirely off the wendigo. I could now move my legs and arms. I wheezed out a breath as pain radiated from my spine, as the bones fused back together.

I precisely knew now the strength of the wendigo now. I had gotten struck by a branch from a tree, which had left me paralyzed, while Finn, in his wendigo form, had the whole damn tree flatten him out yet was already back on his feet.

Sitting up slowly, I watched as the headmistress hissed in pain before she started crashing. However, her injured wings flapped viciously, stopping her four inches above the ground. Then her head was jerked back as she twirled like a fidget spinner. It would have been comical if we were in a different situation. Her black hair was flying all over the place, and she was wrestling with someone who was invisible to her.

The headmistress started throwing punches left and right, and when one finally connected, there was a *thud* as Remy hit the ground. It was then that the headmistress put two and two together. She realized her battle was with a ghost who could not be killed.

"Retreat, Commander."

Actually wanting to obey that command, the wendigo became a storm that I could barely trace as he fled from the woods. The headmistress flew like a broken bird above him. She was wounded but not enough.

I slowly climbed to my feet as Remy appeared in front of me.

"So, I know how this looks."

"It looks like you failed."

"Yeah, again, I know how it looks, but here's the thing. I haven't mastered how to take a life. Killing a fully blessed is a lot different than killing the wendigos. Hindsight, I should have put more juice behind it, but this was a learning experience."

"We're not working on a curve, Remy!"

She crossed her arms over her chest. "Don't get mad at me. *You* should have taken on the headmistress."

I was going to choke her out. "*You think?*" I was fuming mad. "And when she figured out that something was trying to take her life force and took to the sky, how did you get to her? A ley line?"

"No. I'm a ghost, baby. I shimmed up that big oak tree, climbed out on a limb, and jumped. I thought my weight would have her wings tiring out. The problem was that I had to hold onto her pretty hard so I didn't fall, and then I had no hands free to turn her to ash."

"Again, for the people in the cheap seats, she won't turn to ash, Remy. She's not a vampire."

"Okay, stealer of joy. Anything else you want to add to this conversation?"

I rubbed my temples. "Let me think. She might have heard me talking to Finn. Let's assume that she now knows I can turn him back, and if forced, that's exactly what I'll do. She knows that I'm working with a ghost. She won't come back here. She isn't stupid enough to go back to the Empowered Academy, but she needs an army of wendigos."

"Where do you think she'll go now?"

"To be certain, I need to talk with Finn. But if I had to guess, I'd say the headmistress needs to sleep so she can heal. You might not have done what you were supposed to do, but you did hurt her."

Remy buffed her nails on her shirt. "Thanks."

"Finn's wendigo form is way too big for her to carry, so he must travel by foot. I think they are going to get far enough away and hole up somewhere."

Remy worried her bottom lip between her teeth. "So, what's the plan?"

"Wendigo or not, that tree hurt him. I need to sleep and wait for Finn to rest and heal. Then I can dream walk to him. He can tell me exactly where he is, and we can go from there."

Remy picked up a fallen branch that was as big as her arm. "We don't have time for bedtime stories, sugar. The clock is ticking."

"Wha—"

I didn't finish my sentence as the limb came swinging at my face. Remy knocked my ass out.

twenty-eight

IT TOOK ME FOREVER TO find Finn, and when I did, my heart clenched. He looked so forlorn and beaten as he sat on an old stump. His black hair stood up every which way, as if he had been tugging on it, there were shadows under his green eyes, and it looked like he was warring a battle that only he was a part of.

He slowly lifted his face to mine. "I figured you'd come."

I walked toward him slowly then knelt at his feet. Grabbing his face in my hands, I said, "Just hang on. This is almost all over."

"I hurt you," he whispered.

"Please. Don't give yourself too much credit. I hurt myself with that tree more than you hurt me with some hair pulling."

"I still don't like being controlled."

"I know."

He grabbed my wrist and kissed my palm. "The headmistress is healing right now." A smile came upon his face. "Remy damaged one of her wings and did some internal damage. Unfortunately, one of her powers is healing, so she'll be up soon."

"When you are a wendigo, can you see Remy?" I asked.

A handsome smile lit his face. "That was a grade-A shitshow."

I laughed. "Truth. Where are you right now?"

"In a cave on the north side of the mountain."

I nodded.

He squeezed my hand that he still held. "By the time you find us, she'll have moved on. There is a small town at the end of the parkway. She won't be able to hide my form from humans. She'll need to act quickly. My guess is she'll take us somewhere that is still open and try to change as many humans as possible before moving on."

My mouth dropped open. The headmistress was resorting to turning humans. All those innocent people.

"Human wendigos won't be as powerful."

"It won't matter if she has a million in her army, or if you are busy trying to stop the spread, she'll then be able to get into one of the two academies. She just needs to keep you busy." He leaned forward and rested his forehead on mine. "She could use me to infect the entire human population. I would say kill me now, but I'm worried about you facing the original wendigo alone. Then again, what have we accomplished if we are the only two standing at the end of this?"

I jerked back. "Don't talk like that. The whole world could burn before I would even think about ending you."

"You might have to."

"No."

"Gabriella …" He pulled me to my feet then walked around me to pace the length of a well-worn path that was littered with fallen leaves. "Within ten minutes, I could infect thirty humans. Then they could turn around and infect others. We won't be able to stop the spread until every human has turned into a wendigo. You might have found a way to bring the blessed back from a wendigo form, but can you honestly say that you can return a human back to theirs? And you are one person working alone. What you are asking is impossible."

I ignored him. There was no use in arguing with him when I knew I had no intention of ever hurting him. "There is something that I need to tell you. It's about the Flaming Sword."

He stopped pacing. "Everything okay?"

"Better than okay. I got a visit from Uriel. He told me to share the power of the Flaming Sword with six others."

"Were you able to?"

I smiled. "Yes."

"That is amazing! Have the ones you have chosen meet you in the town tonight. There is no way she'll be able to escape all of you. I'll try to withstand her commands for as long as I can."

I winced. "There's a small hiccup in that plan."

He scanned my face. "Define hiccup."

"The ones who now carry part of the power from the Flaming Sword carry a mark that won't allow them to leave the academy."

"So, what is the point of giving them this power?" He stood with his feet shoulder-width apart, arms crossed over his chest, looking every inch the fierce commander he was.

I held his stare that commanded obedience, a gaze that probably would work on anyone other than me. It was laced with hidden depths of immeasurable power. It promised violence to those who didn't comply with his every order. Just the way he carried himself would have a normal person in fight or flight mode, but it created a very different feeling for me—lust.

He shook his head with a smile. "Maka, concentrate."

"Sorry. Once I find the original wendigo that marked the blessed, demis, and prisoners, I'll return him, or her, back to their blessed state. All the people imprisoned at the academy will be free to go, including the ones who now carry the Flaming Sword."

He gave me a nod. "Good. We are going to need all the help we can get. Do you know which wendigo placed the mark?"

This part, I didn't want to tell him, but seeing no other way around it, I said, "I have no clue."

He took the two steps that divided us and grabbed

me by the arms. "Promise me that you won't release the original wendigo unless I'm there."

"Well, it's not like I would know which wendigo is the first. I mean, no offense, but other than weight and height, so far, all of you have looked the same."

"This one will have wings. Non-retractable in the wendigo form. Can't miss them. Now promise me."

My brows clashed. "How do you know this?"

"An archangel visited me."

"Which one?"

He sighed. "Jophiel. Now promise me."

"I promise, I'll wait for you."

He pulled me to him, crushing me to his chest. "I can't live through burying you again."

I rubbed my hands up and down his massive back. "You won't have to." Pulling back from him, I said, "I need you to try to fight against her commands for as long as you can. Walk slow to town. Do everything you can to buy me some time."

"Of course."

He tilted his head toward mine, and when our lips touched, everything in the world seemed a little less complicated. The smell of him wrapped around me, and I instantly committed to memory the taste of him.

He was intoxicating. The more he kissed me, the more I needed him. I gripped him to me as he swirled his tongue with mine. He was irresistible, and I was insatiable. I needed more.

He threaded his hand through my thick hair and wrapped his fist tightly around the long tresses, pulling my head back. He kissed my chin then left a trail of kisses down my throat, making me moan.

"Gabriella," he said between kisses.

"Hmm?"

"When we aren't busy saving humanity and the world, there will be nothing that will stop me from finally claiming you."

He started to pull back, but I grabbed his head and pulled his lips back to my throat. "Claim me now."

He chuckled as he gave me one last kiss. "I don't want to rush through this. The headmistress will be waking up any minute now."

I groaned out loud, though I knew that he was probably right.

"I need to go now, don't I?"

He gave me a smile that the devil himself would be jealous of. It was wicked and full of promises. "If you are going to beat us to the town, you need to hurry."

I rubbed a hand over my chest. "The good news is, if I'm wrong about the destination she picks, then I'll find you. I'll feel you through our bond."

He nodded before he gave me a light push. "Wake up, Maka."

twenty-nine

I SPIT OUT A BIT of dirt as I rolled over and saw Remy was leaning up against a tree. When she noticed me, she came skipping over to me. She braced herself with her hands on her knees as she leaned over me, her hair swinging in her face.

"Yay, you're back. I was so bored."

I glared up at her. "You hit me. Hard."

She nodded as if I was actually asking her a question. "Yep. I'm assuming you talked with the commander?"

I rubbed a hand on the bump on my forehead that was already healing. "Yes."

She stood up and clapped her hands. That damn clapping was going to be the death of me. "You don't have to thank me. So, what did we find out?"

"There is a town near this national park. We need to

find it. Since it will be nightfall, we should focus on the only establishments that are open. She knows that we are on her tail. It would be stupid of her not to hit the biggest gathering she can find."

"So, you think restaurants, movie theatres, bars?"

"Yeah." This was going to be nearly impossible unless we manipulated the odds into our favor. "Go ahead of me and get a lay of the land; see how big the town is."

"Okay. I think you need to fly in with crimson wings and all; make a huge production."

"You want me to fly in and what? Create a panic amongst the humans?"

"Please? Most of them are enamored by the blessed. Go work your magic."

"What and shout something generic like, *Run to your homes, lock the doors, call your loved ones, or kiss your asses goodbye?* I'm completely paraphrasing what I think the inside of your mind is like right now, but am I close?"

She shrugged. "I mean, maybe amp up the theatrics a bit, but yeah, along those lines."

"Yeah, so here's the thing. What's going to happen when the headmistress shows up and it's a ghost town? She will know that something is up. What if she then decides to go to the next town or the next state? We will never find her."

"Okay, I'll be thinking of something else."

"How about, right now, you go scout the town, and I'll meet you on Main Street. Then we can plan."

She was gone before I had my wings out.

I flew to the sky in a blur of red. My heart felt lighter up in the air, and I instantly thought of Hannah. So far, her loss had been more significant than any of ours. As soon as I had the headmistress taken care of, I would make sure to spend time with her.

I had landed quietly outside the city limits in hopes that no one would notice me. At this point, the back of my shirt was so torn and shredded from where my wings came out that I was scared I would be showing so major side boob. I took the torn ends at the bottom and tied it back, hoping my shirt would pass for a halter top. Then there were my jeans, which were muddy and torn at the knees from wrestling with a wendigo. However, I would rather everyone think I'm a runaway teenager than a fully blessed.

Once I got to a neighborhood, I realized that it was exactly what people thought of me. Some gave me pitying looks, and some made sure not to make eye contact. After walking a couple of miles toward town, I found a little girl's bike propped up against a mailbox. It had a pink basket in the front and streamers hanging down the handlebars. I went around the side of the house and found the child playing jump rope.

Trying to give her a smile that wasn't creepy, I said, "Hi."

She immediately stopped jumping and looked at me with a funny look on her face. Maybe I missed the mark on the smile. "My mother is right inside," she told me snottily.

"Cool. So, I need to meet my friend in town, and I don't have a way. Would it be okay if I borrowed your bike?"

She squinted at me. "Um, no. First off, you're too old for my bike. Like you're so old you should be driving. Secondly, how do I know you will return my bike?"

"Those are all valid questions, in which I have zero answers for."

That made her smile. "I don't like Colton."

I looked around the empty yard. "I'm sorry. What was that again?"

She rolled her eyes. "Colton. He's in my fifth-grade class. He is mean, but he's also the teacher's son, so he gets away with it."

I started to back away. I didn't know what possessed me to ask if I could borrow the bike in the first place. I had never stolen anything in my life but, considering I was potentially saving the world, I should be able to cut myself some slack.

"Anyway, I can't stand him. He lives next door." She pointed at the two-story house right next to hers. "He's at church. Yep, on a Wednesday. He is so bad that he needs two days a week to fess up to his sins. Right now, he is probably having people pray for his soul."

I waved, hoping it would get her to stop talking. "Well, it was nice to meet you."

"His bike is in the shed. It's a ten-speed, and Colton is

tall for his age, so if you steal it, you won't look like such a loser when you're biking around town."

I smiled at her as I headed to the house next door. "Thanks!"

She picked up her jump rope. "No, thank you. And just remember, snitches end in ditches."

My smile faltered a little. When did children turn so savage?

I gave her another wave as I ran to the shed. Finding the bike, I hopped on, thanking Colton for being large for his age so I didn't look like a clown as I peddled down the road as fast as I could.

I passed a few homes scattered here and there, along with a few fliers for the watermelon festival that began tonight at six and would last until Sunday. This wasn't good. A festival would be outdoors. Not in a place where we could contain wendigos.

I found Remy sitting on a bench, watching the cars go by on Main Street's curvy road. She held an ice cream cone as she basked in the sun.

"Where did you get that?" I asked as I pointed at the vanilla dripping down her hand.

"I'm a ghost. I can zip into any store and take what I want. And Mama needed some ice cream, especially after I just found out how screwed we really are."

Glad to know one of us didn't have issues with stealing.

She narrowed her eyes at me for a second. "And where did you get that?"

I put the kickstand down as I got off the bike. "I borrowed it from a bully named Colton, who is at church, repenting for his sins. And what do you mean exactly by *we're screwed*? Are you talking about the festival?"

She licked her cone. "Yep. The whole town is shutting down for this festival. They have an outdoor fair and everything. Tonight starts off the festival with a jalapeño eating contest. Don't ask me why these humans would punish themselves like that, but let them live while they can. Half the town will probably be wendigos by the end of the night."

"Not helping," I snapped. "Where does this festival take place exactly?"

"Two streets down. They have the road closed from there until fifth street. So, that's an area of five blocks to cover."

I groaned. "I'll find a rooftop somewhere in the middle of the street, hide out there, and wait."

She ate her ice cream leisurely like we had all the time in the world. "I'll go in ghost form when I'm done. You know, there is no way we are going to be able to save these people."

"I don't know what other choices we have."

She gave me a steady look. "This is why I'm the best friend. Anyone else would convince you to take the commander out. Or worse, change him back to the blessed, possibly causing your death. Instead, I'm going to sit here, enjoy the sun beating down on me while I eat this delicious vanilla ice cream, and take one last look at the world as we know it before it's overrun with wendigos."

I rolled my eyes. "You are so dramatic. We are not going to let the headmistress turn the town into wendigos."

"Well, either way, today should be interesting."

"Do check-ins with me. This time, if you find the headmistress first, let me handle it. We can't afford for her to escape again."

Another lick. "My pleasure. Wielding the Flaming Sword on such a big fish in my first rodeo was too much pressure, to be honest with you. This whole situation has my anxiety level so high."

I watched as she waved at someone walking by like she was one of the locals. If this was her stressed, I had no words for when she relaxed.

I ran a hand over my chest. "I don't feel Finn. He isn't anywhere close. I'm going to go walk Main Street and get a feel for the activities for tonight."

She stood up, finishing her ice cream. "I'll come, too. You know, this is a cute little town."

She stopped an elderly gentleman who was walking his dog on the sidewalk. "Excuse me, sir. Me and my friend are visiting your lovely little town. What is the population here?"

He beamed. "We're up to ten thousand." He then went on to tell us the brief history of the town and the founding fathers, who happened to be one of his third cousins, twice removed.

Remy tipped an imaginary hat to him. "Thank you so

much for the history lesson."

He waved us off, and I sighed.

"Ten thousand is a tiny population."

"Yeah, but it's the beginning of a great army."

I nodded. If Finn was unable to control himself until we could find him, we were screwed. All of us.

thirty

RIGHT IN FRONT OF THE courthouse, there was a stage set up. Four guys, all middle-aged, were rocking out to some southern rock song. The lead singer thought God had given him a talent that he needed to share with the world, or at least this small town, and his friends, neighbors, and the town residents didn't have the heart to tell him that he was tone-deaf.

Remy cheered after their first song was over. "I wonder if they take recommendations?"

"I'll kill you," I said as I looked up and down the narrow, curvy street. "It looks like they have already closed the businesses on this street for the festival's kick-off."

Remy pointed to a few pop-up tents. "It looks like the local restaurants are working from those tents." Her nose curled up when she picked up a flyer. "With a limited menu."

244

"Good thing we're not here for music or food."

"Joy killer. It looks like they are finishing setting up a small fair on the last two blocks."

"So, on these five blocks, we have a fair for children, food stations, lemonade, funnel cakes, and caramel apples, along with a whole booth for watermelons. If the headmistress has Finn attack one human at a time, it will cause everyone to panic and run. She needs to hit as many as possible, and I would think she wouldn't do it in broad daylight in the middle of the street."

As we walked toward the fair, I found a carnival house had set up. There was a sign out front that stated you had to be eighteen years or older, or accompanied by a parent, in order to go into the carnival house."

"Winner, winner chicken dinner," Remy said.

"Yeah, it looks like her best bet."

"Great." Remy clapped. "So glad we narrowed down where she'd probably go on these measly five blocks. I'm going to help myself to some watermelon and flirt with the lemonade stand guy. Since I'm newly single, he can be my rebound."

I gave her a what-the-hell look.

She shrugged. "Listen, I'm not an expert on the language of love, but one thing I do know is there are a lot of fish in the sea. The ocean is a charcuterie board of men from goldfish to Moby Dicks. Men are like trains; if you stand there long enough, another one will be by in a second. All aboard!"

I shook my head as she started swinging her hips as she walked to the lemonade stand. Then I sat on the curb, waiting for my heartstrings to tighten. The hot temperatures began to cool as the sun went down. Townsfolk laughed and talked with people who they ran into on the street. Children begged their parents to buy them a ticket to the inflatables that were set up in the fair section. The festival was everything one would think it would be—laughter, music, and a good time. I thought maybe we were all wrong, and the headmistress had decided against stopping at this little town when, all of a sudden, I felt him. Finn was getting closer.

I rushed over to find Remy. She was eating a funnel cake and talking with an elderly woman.

"Excuse us," I said as I pulled Remy away.

Remy shouted over her shoulder, "Make sure you rest that knee, Mary Kate."

Then she whispered to me, "That woman has so much topical pain relief ointment on her body that I'll never get the smell out of my nostrils."

"Remy, Finn is getting closer."

She chucked the remainder of her funnel cake into a trash bin. "Okay. It makes sense. It's almost dark. What do you want me to do?"

"Can you look above, and when you see which way they are heading, let me know?"

She nodded.

"I think I'll go into the carnival house and wait there.

It's dark, and she'll be able to hide the ones that Finn turns into wendigos there."

"Before I go all ghost, I'll create a distraction for you."

"What?"

"You don't have tickets, sugar dumpling. How are you going to get in? Show 'em a little nip?"

"Ew. Gross. No."

She rolled her blue eyes. "Didn't think so, my prudish friend. I'll help you out. Plus, it didn't work out with the lemonade guy."

I scoffed. "What? He wasn't impressed by you?"

"The gay ones never are, babe." She pushed me to the side of the carnival house. "There is an opening in the flap of the tent. I'll flirt with the guy until you're in."

"Thanks," I said.

"No worries. I'm best friend material; I can't help but be superb."

I was laughing as I slipped into the tent. The next hour would either go incredibly well, or it would be the beginning of the end.

I took calming breaths as Finn grew closer and closer.

From where I hid behind a funny mirror, I could hear a gaggle of teenagers outside. They must have been lining up.

It was about five minutes away from complete darkness when I felt a tightness close in around me. Finn was right outside. He must be at the side flap where I had entered.

A gust of cold air rushed over me before I heard Remy say, "She is twenty feet away. Right outside this tent, there is an old building that's a general store. Down the side is a dumpster. Look behind it."

"If Finn loses the war within himself, do whatever you can to stop him without killing him."

"You got it."

I brushed past my friend and the cold air that surrounded her to see a wendigo's reflection in the funny mirrors. He made eye contact with me, and I could tell the man trapped inside was doing everything he could to slow down time.

I ran out of the tent and toward the narrow brick building. The headmistress heard me and, as I approached the dumpster before I could reach her, she punched her wings out and took to the sky. Without hesitation, I immediately followed her.

The moment she caught sight of my crimson wings, her mouth dropped open. Her shock allowed me time to catch her.

We spun like a torpedo above the fair. The farther I got her away, the less of a hold she had over Finn. She struggled against me, but it was pointless. I wasn't letting her go. I wrapped my legs around her waist like a python as my wings continued to spiral us upward. I could no longer see anyone from below. Even the tents looked tiny from how high we were.

"Let me go," she snarled.

I was bitter and angry for what she had done to Finn, Hannah, and so many countless others. The anger burned in me bright with a fire that was escaping me. Without even touching her with my palms, light poured out of me, lighting up the night sky. I pushed that light toward her.

"I am the judge, jury, and executioner. Your time here on earth is done."

She let out a scream before she went limp.

I released her from my thighs then watched as she plummeted to the ground. Slowly descending between the buildings, I stopped to look at the headmistress lying there, bloody and broken on the ground. Her wings had turned to ash, and her lifeless eyes stared up into the night sky. Leaving her body there, I ran back to the carnival tent.

Slipping inside the side flap, I found Remy standing in front of the wendigo. She had backed him behind a light-up skull that was in the corner.

The humans were completely unaware that they weren't alone while standing on a gravity-powered tipping floor in front of a dark corridor. The teenage boys laughed as the girls with them clung to their arms while screaming.

Quietly, I walked toward Finn, who took a step back.

I heard Remy whisper, "Easy, big guy."

I held my hand to him. After a moment of hesitation, he took it. Then I led them out to the darkness outside.

"I think I can carry him."

"But how?"

"My wings might not be as massive as the other fully blessed—at least not that I've seen—but I had no issue holding the headmistress up in the air."

"Yeah, well, no offense, but the headmistress was a lot

smaller than the commander. I can say past tense, right?"

I nodded. "You'll be happy to know that her wings actually did turn to ash."

Remy pumped her fist in the air. "Knew it."

"We need to hurry before anyone finds the body."

Once again, my wings came out as I put my arms around the wendigo's waist. "Hold on to me."

Finn obeyed as we shot up in the air.

It was definitely harder. My back muscles quickly began to ache, and sweat dripped from my brow. I barely made it outside of the town limits before I had to stop. As soon as my feet touched the ground in the woods, I released my hold on the wendigo. Then I took a few steps and landed on my knees. I barely had the energy to retract my wings.

Clammy hands wrapped around me, swinging me up into their arms. I stared up into the soulless eyes of the wendigo, knowing that Finn was in there somewhere. Without thought, I rested my head against his pale, veiny chest.

Remy appeared a few seconds later. "Hey, lost you guys." She scanned us over. "This should be extremely creepy, but I'm enough of a weirdo that I can say, whatever floats your boat."

I was exhausted. Besides the cat naps that consisted of a few minutes here and there over the last week, I had received very little sleep. My adrenaline had left me. So, now that I knew the headmistress could no longer control Finn, a deep sleep took me under. I would deal with the issues of the marked and the other wendigos when I woke.

thirty-one

FINN WORE A COME-HITHER SMILE, one that any woman over the age of eighteen and under seventy couldn't ignore.

My feet carried me the short distance to him as I looked around at our scenery. We were under the night sky. Every star twinkled brightly as crickets made a musical symphony all around us. The grass lightly tickled my ankles.

"Did I dream walk to you?"

He nodded. "We're close to the Empowered Academy. Remy insisted that we stop and take a break. The truth is that I think she is scared to show up with you unconscious in a wendigo's arms, but she didn't want to admit that. Neither one of us wanted to wake you up either. You haven't been sleeping well, Maka."

I rubbed a hand over my face. "Considering what has

251

been going on, sleep had to take a backseat."

"I'm proud of you."

"Thanks."

He reached out and took my hands in his. We both tilted our heads back and looked at the night sky. These rare moments of just quietness and togetherness were so far and few between that I wanted to stay here all night.

He looked down at me with a half-grin.

I raised my eyebrows. "What?"

"I can feel your happiness."

"Can we just chill here for a while?"

He shook his head. "While I'm away from the Academy of Seraph, I'm leaving it vulnerable. And, while the headmistress's death was a huge feat, it's only the beginning of what we need to accomplish."

I groaned as my head hit his chest. "Will it always be like this?"

With his warm hands, he rubbed my back. "Life is hard. Even if we take the easiest paths possible, life is hard. Might as well decide the paths we want to take from the beginning. Right now, you are saving hundreds of people from imprisonment. You are freeing the blessed from dark magic forms that they didn't deserve or ask for. You've given the students and faculty of the Empowered Academy a new option—to join society or enroll at the Academy of Seraph. You are doing big things. Things that will help pave a path to fighting bigger adversaries than the headmistress."

I sighed. "Thanks. I needed that pep talk."

His chest rumbled. "Anytime, Maka, anytime. You ready to wake up and get back to work?"

"No, not really, but you're right. Can you just hold me for a few more minutes?"

"There is nothing in this world that I'd rather do."

I closed my eyes and rested against the man that I loved. I didn't know what the remainder of tonight or tomorrow would bring, but knowing that the headmistress was one less thing I had to worry about had me relaxing.

I listened to Finn's heartbeat and snuggled deeper into him. I couldn't worry about the future. It was the right now that counted, and right now, was pretty damn awesome.

Remy gave me two hours of sleep before she was half on top of me, shaking me awake. Since she had made us a makeshift camp right outside of the academy, our journey forward wouldn't be too long.

Walking back into the Empowered Academy with a huge-ass wendigo was comical. Some people ran, others took fighting stances, and a woman fainted. The animals patrolling the border growled at Finn.

Calling them to me, I commended them all for doing such an excellent job of protecting the academy. A snake slithered against my ankle, and I smiled as Remy screamed, "Voodoo shit!" before walking twenty feet ahead of me. I pet some deer and coyotes.

"Stay and eat or leave if you want." My voice hummed with power. "Thank you so much for everything." I smiled as a family of foxes ran down the mountain. I could just imagine them chasing each other in the lavender field.

I glanced beside me to see the wendigo with a stoic look on his face. Come to think about it, that was the only facial expression that they owned.

We entered the school entrance, where more students screamed or ran. Remy seemed to be taking a perverse satisfaction out of the startled students. I gave her a look as I closed the door behind us.

During all the commotion, Luna showed up. Her pink hair bounced around her in a cloud as she skipped every other step down the steps. She gave me a stiff wave as she eyed the wendigo looming over me. "Hi. So, I'm assuming this large creature is Finn."

Remy snorted. "In the pale, veiny flesh."

"Yep, and if we could get him out of view, that would be great." I eyed a chunky kid to the side of us. His eyes were narrowed into slits as he stared at us. "I have a feeling we are not warmly accepted right now."

Luna nodded. "Of course. Let's um ... go to the gymnasium. Trev and Ezra are there with Hannah. She has been doing great, by the way. She turned back seven wendigos to their blessed form. So far, she has been able to turn more back than any of us without tiring, minus you, of course."

"Really?" I asked as we followed behind Luna.

Students were getting out of our way in fear that the wendigo would get too close. Some more daring students gathered around on the stairwell. Their mouths were hung open, and they were in awe that the wendigo was following behind us.

"Yeah. I didn't know your friend before she came here, but I can tell you that she is an amazing person. Resilient. She tries hard and has a great attitude. I'm glad that she is allowing me into her life. Friends, at least true friends, are rare to come by, and what I've seen so far from Hannah, she is a jewel in the midst of cubic zirconia."

I smiled at her accurate description of my friend. Hannah was one of a kind.

Luna threw the golden doors open, and I stepped into the room with Remy and my wendigo trailing behind.

Ezra was covering a human up with a blanket when he noticed us. His movements stalled for a minute before he stood and fully took in the situation. "That's one huge son of a—"

"Yep," I interrupted. "This is Finn. Let's all try to keep in mind that, while he is in this form, he must continually fight against his emotions."

"A wendigo's emotions are too kill or convert," Ezra said.

I nodded. "Right, so we need to be mindful of how we talk around—"

Finn roared as he saw Trev approach the group.

Trev jumped back with his hands up in surrender.

"What the hell is going on, guys?"

Finn was growing more and more agitated.

"Apparently, he has some unresolved issues with you kidnapping me. Right now is not the best time to work those out. I need to take him to my room."

"That's a bad idea," Ezra said. "There are students here who will grow quite upset with a wendigo residing right next to them."

I grabbed the wendigo's arm. "I don't care how upset people get."

Trev had backed almost all the way out of the room, and Luna had stepped in front of him to try to get the wendigo's attention off of him, but so far, it wasn't working. At this point, Finn was having a hard time controlling his form. His black eyes were narrowed on Trev, and like a dog with a bone, he wasn't letting go. He shrugged out of my grip way too easily and started stalking his prey.

"Just for now," Remy started, "maybe we should take him to the cell that you were in."

I cut my gaze to her.

"Just for now. Think about it. Everyone will feel safer, and if something happens like this"—she motioned to Trev and how there were four of us now between Finn and Trev, who was backed up to the golden door—"we won't have to worry about him snapping."

I put a hand on the wendigo's chest. "Finn, I know that you are still in there. Back up."

The wendigo didn't look at me but continued to snarl

at Trev.

"Trev, leave," I barked.

We all shoved forward so Trev had enough room to open the door. As soon as he was gone, the wendigo quieted down, and we all breathed a little easier.

I patted the milky white flesh of the wendigo. "All right, big guy, let's get you settled below."

Remy gave me a nod. She knew that I didn't want Finn stuck in a cell, but the truth was, while he was in this form, he *was* a wendigo. The man I loved might be fighting his natural desires while a wendigo, but at the end of the day, he was just that—a wendigo.

I started to pull Finn through the golden doors, but he wouldn't budge. He threw my arm off and stalked toward the glass doors, where he paced in front of them.

"He doesn't want to leave if he thinks we are going to convert more wendigos into the blessed," I said to no one in particular. "He is convinced that I will die if he isn't here to protect me."

"Then he stays," Hannah stated simply.

Trev opened the golden doors and barely poked his head in. "Why isn't he coming out?"

"Change of plans, brother," Ezra said. "The wendigo stays."

I walked to the glass doors and pulled Finn to the side. "Can you sit here and not interfere unless you are needed?"

When the wendigo tilted his head, the veins on his neck were more pronounced through his pale skin. Black, soulless eyes that I was pretty sure were incapable of blinking stared at me for what seemed like forever. Finally, the wendigo went to the wall and crouched down.

I gave him a nod. "Make yourself comfortable. We will be here for a while."

I walked back to the group by the golden doors. "Come in, Trev."

Luna opened the door. "I suggest going nowhere near that wendigo."

Trev shrugged like it wasn't that big of a deal. "I have the Flaming Sword in me."

"I wouldn't be too overconfident. I believe that Finn is powerful enough that he could make the Flaming Sword combust inside of us."

Luna looked over at the crouched wendigo that looked like a gargoyle ready to take flight at any minute and cleared her throat. "Do you think the dream you talked about ... the one where it was predicted that a wendigo would almost be your undoing ... do you think it's him?"

Remy shook her head. "No way. If it were Finn in that prediction, he would have allowed Gabriella to turn him back into the blessed. I think he is going to be her saving grace."

"All of our saving graces," I said.

Ezra shuddered. "I really don't like being saved, but if I must, I'd prefer it to be some hot woman, not ... you know." He looked over at the wendigo. "No offense, man."

"Can he actually understand us?" Trev asked.

Remy sighed. "So hot when they aren't talking."

I couldn't help the laughter that poured out of me. If humanity could see that this group of teenagers was in charge of saving the world, they would go ahead and call their priests to have their last rites said over them.

After a few minutes, we decided which pair was going to work on the wendigos first. It was agreed that, no matter what, I was to stay inside the gymnasium just in case I needed to calm Finn down.

We all worked tirelessly with one goal in mind—free the blessed and don't get killed in the process. Each of us understood that Camaella was on her way to the Academy of Seraph. We had to hurry if we had any hopes of going up against her and her army of demons.

thirty-two

DAY FIVE STARTED LIKE THE last four but took a turn for the worst. The academy understood that no one was allowed, other than the six of us, in the gymnasium, so when a young freshman burst through the doors, we were all startled.

The wendigo that Luna had been converting got around her in her distraction and was heading toward the doors. Ezra was running for the wendigo as I was throwing the startled freshman out of the way when the wendigo was tackled to the ground by a sandstorm of power. Finn snarled and punched the wendigo as if my life depended on it.

I tried to stop him. "Finn, let go. I've got this."

After the fourth hit, I put my body between the wendigo and Finn's fist. The air in the room changed when Finn punched the ground next to my head. I stared up into the

massive wendigo's black eyes as I watched it fight to get back in control.

"Finn, I know you are in there, and I need you to listen to me. Please. Thank you for helping us, but I need you to stop now. I can't change the wendigo back into the blessed if you kill him, or her, first." I watched as he took deep breaths. He was in there, and he was fighting. I reached up and laid a hand on the wendigo's cheek. "Thank you for helping me, but I got this."

The wendigo underneath me started fighting for control, causing Finn to struggle.

"Go over to your corner, Finn." Not waiting to see if he did or not, I rolled over, basically laying on top of the wendigo. Ezra had one arm pinned down with his boot heel, and Luna was kneeling on the other arm.

I placed my palm on the wendigo and waited for it to warm. Once the wendigo stopped struggling, I said, "Give it a blanket."

When Luna jumped up to get one, I turned to the freshman who was white as a sheet. His hair stuck up every which way, and his too big clothes hung on his small frame. His dilated pupils, along with his irregular breathing, suggested that he was in shock, but I didn't care.

"What the hell do you think you were doing?" I asked. "Did you not understand the first three times that we told everyone in this academy that they were not to come in this room?"

Ezra came up beside me. "You better have a damn good

excuse as to why you are in here."

We watched as the boy's mouth opened and closed and his eyes went to the corner where Finn was pacing beside the glass doors.

Getting in his space, I said, "Eyes on me. You have three seconds to tell me why you are here."

"I'm … I'm sorry," he said. "I had a dream, and it was so real that I thought I should tell someone."

I put my hands on my hips. "A dream?"

"Well, no, not really."

Finn made a sound somewhere behind me that sounded like a roar.

"Which was it? A dream or not? Spit it out," I said.

"Maybe I shouldn't have come here," the boy said.

"You think?" Ezra snapped. "What's your name?"

"Kota."

My patience was waning. We had so many more wendigos that needed to be changed and not enough time. "Kota, tell me about this dream of yours."

He nodded. "Sometimes, I see things that are like flashes, but they aren't really dreams. I don't know how to describe them." He was rambling.

Grabbing his arm, I closed my eyes as I tried to pick up on what he had seen. My power swirled around me then toward Kota as it gently attempted to pluck the information that I needed from him.

I saw him standing in the cafeteria line. He was making jokes with his only, and best, friend when the tray slipped from his hands. Visions of a beautiful fallen angel came into his mind. She had an army behind her as she visited with the Prince of Darkness. The meeting left her feeling desperate. She was running out of time. That was … until she found out about the wendigos that the headmistress had made. It seemed that, even in death, Mrs. Fields wasn't done with her treachery.

Before coming to the Empowered Academy to try to negotiate with the headmistress, she had sent a letter to be delivered to Camaella, sort of as a backup plan. The letter hadn't saved Mrs. Fields, but it had created a hell of a problem for us. Camaella wanted these wendigos.

Supposed she had these beasts along with the demons, Camaella could go up against the commander at the Academy of Seraph. She would have the Flaming Sword. I watched as she marched with her army here, to this academy.

Letting go of Kota, I stumbled back. "Go get the others, Ezra."

He gave me a worried glance but did as I asked.

Kota was looking at me in awe. "Did you see what I saw? How did you do that?"

"Kota, coming to me was the right thing to do, even if it was incredibly stupid. Go find your family. Spend time with them and don't say a word about this to anyone." Before he could leave, I snagged his arm again. "I mean it, Kota. You will only cause a kind of panic that I don't have time to deal with at the moment. Can I count on you?"

He swallowed nervously before he said, "Of course." Then he ran out of the golden doors, letting them bang closed behind him.

"How screwed are we?" Luna asked.

"The kind of screwed where I would tell a freshman to go spend some time with his family screwed."

She winced. "That's what I thought."

A young girl was lying on the floor with a towel thrown over her. Guessed we were running out of blankets. Luna went over to her and started explaining what had just happened.

I searched out the tall wendigo in the corner and rubbed a hand over my chest. Anger and frustration were coming through. I wasn't sure if I was picking up on Finn's emotions or if it was me who was emitting those feelings. My guess was both. I was pretty angry that we couldn't seem to catch a break, and I was frustrated that yet another psycho had thwarted our plans.

I waited until all five of the people I had chosen to carry the Flaming Sword had come in. Then, without letting them talk, I said, "Guys, we have a problem." I explained that a young but apparently up-and-coming kid had picked up on a vision of Camaella. I told them exactly what I saw, and then I waited … waited for one of them to say something.

Hannah said, "Do we have a timeframe on when she will arrive?"

"From the vision that I saw, she will be passing over a

town. The day that she goes through, it was decorated with hearts."

"Valentine's Day," Remy said.

"Yeah."

Trev swore. "That's in two days. You have got to be kidding me."

None of us spoke. We all let the magnitude of what was about to happen hit us like a ton of bricks.

Luna ran a hand through her pink hair. "Break down our options for us."

Before I could say anything, Trev said, "The three of you will have to leave us—Remy, Hannah, and Gabriella. Make a run for it, and we will try to fend her off from as long as we can."

My two best friends stood there beside me, giving Trev the same look as I was.

"Um … we don't run," Remy said.

Hannah shook her head. "I'm marked, too, remember? That wouldn't matter, though. Even without my wings, I am more powerful than my family ever thought I'd be, and my power is growing. I can feel it. If archangels chose Gabriella, and she chose us, what would it make us to turn our backs on the people who are trapped here and can't leave?"

"Cowards," I said. "And I can assure you that we aren't weak."

"Hell no," Remy said.

Ezra gave Remy a wink. "Are you sure you want to call the wedding off?"

She rolled her eyes. "That ship has sailed, lover boy."

"Now that we know that the two of us aren't planning on deserting all of you here," I said, "we only have one option."

"To fight?" Luna asked.

"No," I said. "We can't take the chance of going up against them. What if they get past us and allow the wendigos out? Think of the damage they could do to the ones here who are held prisoner. Plus, with Camaella working hand-in-hand with the Prince of Darkness, I don't know if they know how to control the wendigos. Our only option is to get everyone out of here."

"How will we remove their marks?" Remy asked.

"*We* won't," I said. "*I* will. This is what is going to happen. I have a day to get to the original wendigo."

Trev scoffed. "You are going into the plane to find the original? Are you crazy?"

I narrowed my eyes at him. "If I don't do this, who will you lose, Trev? Think of the twins. They are sitting ducks here. This is the only way."

The wendigo had stopped pacing. I noticed that Finn was now staring at me.

Giving my attention to my friends, I said, "I'm going down there. Hopefully, Finn will agree to go with me. I need him to block as many wendigos from me as possible. I'll find the original—the one with black wings. If I can free her, it will release the mark and the remainder of the wendigos. This is the only chance we have of beating the clock."

Remy nodded. "We will all go with you."

I shook my head. "No. I need you guys to stay here just in case I don't make it back. The five of you will be the only hope all of these people have against Camaella."

Tears ran down Remy's face while Hannah gave me a terse nod. It was incredible how much Hannah had grown in strength. A few weeks ago, she would have been the one standing in front of me, crying.

Remy said, "This is suicide. You will be going against roughly eight hundred or so wendigos. Remember what the archangel said when she visited you in that dream? You will combust. No one can take on that many wendigos. We should go with you."

"All of us stand to lose something if I don't make it back," I said. "I'm hoping that Finn will keep the majority away from me. Of course I want you to go, but you can't. Not this time. You are needed here."

Every single one of them gave me an emotional hug goodbye. When Trev wrapped me up in a hug, there was a snarl before his feet left the floor and he went flying through the air. The wendigo towering above me made an inhuman sound while his nostrils flared in displeasure.

"Dude, kind of had that coming," Remy said.

Trev made his way back to his feet. "I was just telling her good luck and goodbye."

When the wendigo took another step toward Trev, I put myself between the both of them. Commandeering the wendigo's attention, I said, "I need to get in that plane.

Do you think you can help me find the original?"

In answer, he turned and strolled toward the glass doors.

Before my friends could wrap me in another tearful goodbye, I followed my wendigo, wiping the sweat from my palms as Trev and Ezra opened the doors. As soon as they hit the button, we would jump into the unknown without hesitation.

It seemed like time dragged by when, finally, a tiny space on the floor opened up. Without thinking, I jumped. If I was honest, I could have sworn, with certainty, that Finn had enough control over the wendigo to make him jump into a place where the wendigos obviously detested.

When I felt my wendigo's body next to mine as we fell down a set of steps that were in the pitch black, I sagged with relief. There was no way I could do this independently, but with Finn, I stood a chance. There was no doubt that we were about to go through hell, but there was no one else in the world that I would rather travel the shadows of darkness with. I just prayed we would both make it out of the valley.

thirty-three

I TRIED MY HARDEST TO control my breathing but being submerged in the dark with wendigos lurking in the shadows wasn't the best feeling in the world. I felt clammy hands brush by my arm and jumped a little before I realized that Finn was telling me that I needed to keep moving.

At first, none of the wendigos came close to us, but the farther we went through what looked like a subway tunnel, the less shy they became. I would try my hardest not to use my power, needing to save it.

Every wendigo that got too close was thrown by my wendigo. He was doing a great job of not letting them near, but the farther we went, the more obvious it was that he couldn't keep that up forever. We were sorely outnumbered.

A pack of wendigos rushed us, and Finn became a

sandstorm as he threw them this way and that. One of the wendigos grabbed a fistful of my hair and started dragging me away from Finn and the battle he was in. If he did that, I was done for. Without Finn's protection, I had to use the power inside of me.

Palm out, I ignited the wendigo and watched as it fell to the ground. Strong arms wrapped around me. I didn't fight or resist as the wendigo shielded me from the onslaught of other wendigos crowding around us. Pushing me forward, he blocked the hands reaching out for me.

Luckily, the passageway was narrowing as we went farther through the plane. Finn slashed his claws at all that were before us and took the brunt of the ones that were behind us.

Once the tunnel branched off and became more expansive at the elbow of the tunnel, we took the right path, which led to a dead-end filled only with wendigos. Backtracking was exhausting, and when we came back to the crossroads, we went left this time. Unfortunately, a small group was waiting for us, and I had to use my powers for the second time.

There was a steady rhythm of dripping with every step we took. Looking down, I saw blood splatter the thick concrete floors. My wendigo's back was in some serious bad shape.

Hurrying down the tunnel, I asked, "Are you okay?"

Of course, he didn't answer. I wasn't sure if Finn was struggling more for control now that he was wounded. I silently wondered how much pain a wendigo felt and how fast they healed. If we both made it out of this alive, I would be sure to ask Finn.

Dodging the grasps of wendigos, we trudged forward through the dark tunnel. Every once in a while, the tunnel would widen, and we would pick up the pace through the sections, careful not to drain too much power.

Eventually, I thought we had come up to yet another dead end, but when I went to turn around, Finn blocked me and forced me to take steps backward in the narrow tunnel. My feet almost tripped over a hinge. Looking down, I saw a grate in the ground.

Wendigos were crowding in behind him. At this point, we couldn't go back the way we had come. There were too many of them.

I lifted the grate and stared into the black abyss. It was either drop into a hole and pray it led somewhere or die trying to return back through the tunnel. So, I plunged into the darkness with Finn coming in right behind me, having closed the grate as he fell. I honestly didn't think that would deter the other wendigos for too long.

The drop was nine feet into a pit. The rock walls almost had a bluish glow to them. The rock and dirt floor had a similar sheen, like magical glow worms had left a trail going every which way. I cringed as I heard the grate clang. There would be a horde of wendigos on us in no time.

My gut told me that we were in grave danger, and my heartbeat sped up as I ignored the warning signs, because there, against the wall, was a chained wendigo.

Unlike all the other wendigos, its skin wasn't pale but dark, like its eyes. This was the original?

I walked forward, ready to end this all when, with one tug, the wendigo broke through the chains that must have been there for show. Well, that wasn't good. I knew I couldn't get near the original. It would kill me before I could touch it.

Wendigos began flooding the room as I watched the original stretch its wings out. They were black and shiny. Magnificent.

Finn was a sandstorm of motion as he whirled around the onslaught of incoming wendigos

Calling my power to me, I braced myself, but before I could send my light toward it, a wendigo sideswiped me, knocking me to the ground. Placing my palm on the wendigo, I used my power again.

Getting to my feet, I saw hundreds of wendigos packed into the room but not the original. *Shit.*

As hands grabbed me, I realized they were trying to turn me, and once that didn't happen, they became more agitated. I stayed on my feet as long as I could, but the moment they took me to the ground, I knew I was in trouble.

My power was flowing out of me. I had used it nine times before I could finally get to my feet. Wendigos were hitting the rock walls as the sandstorm flew by them. More wendigos were upon me, but I knew I couldn't call for Finn. He was doing his part. I had to stay on my feet. It was the only way that I would survive.

I caught a glimpse of black wings and ran toward where we had first dropped into this shithole. More wendigos were falling in at an alarming rate. We were so screwed.

My palms heated as I had to use my power again and again. The sandstorm came and blocked for me. I had used my power twenty-two times now. My legs were shaking, and I felt like I would vomit at any second, but I kept putting one foot in front of the other. I had to get to the original.

Right before it started to fly upward through the grate, my wendigo tackled the original to the ground.

Breaking out of a wendigos' hold, I stumbled forward and threw my body half on top of the original and half on top of Finn, who was wrestling with the original. A calmness entered my soul as a light burst through me to the original.

I chanted silently, "Don't kill. Please turn back. Please release these people," as black dots swam in my vision and blood started to pour out of my nose. I knew I was in danger, but I had to turn the wendigo back. I had made a promise to Sandalphon, one I intended to keep.

Pushing more light at the original, I prayed that we both would make it.

My ears began to ring as my wendigo grabbed my arm. Finn was snarling at me. I was dying.

All of a sudden, everything quieted. There was no noise as a warm feeling coated my whole body. A warm liquid fell all over me before there was nothing more.

thirty-four

JOPHIEL STOOD BEFORE ME. HER light brown skin glistened in the sunlight as she grabbed her white dress and twirled around in circles. Her laughter was so beautiful that it became contagious. I laughed as I walked toward her.

She bent down and picked a handful of daisies. Bringing them to her beautiful face, she inhaled like she wanted to remember that smell for the rest of her life. Then she stood up and tilted her head at me before she ran to me and pulled me in her arms, hugging me so tightly I could barely breathe. Like a kid on Christmas, she released me and bounced on her feet with anticipation and joy.

"Gabriella, look," she said as she waved her arms around her. "Miles and miles of my favorite flowers. Do you feel the warmth of the sun?"

I nodded. "Yes, it's beautiful here. But … where is here?"

She giggled. "When you die, your brain carries you away to a place that comforts you."

My mouth dropped open. "We're dead?"

"Almost, love, almost."

I looked around at the beautiful scenery. There wasn't a cloud in the sky, and the warm sun beat down on the daisy fields. Butterflies landed on flowers, and birds sang a beautiful tune nearby. I didn't want to be here.

I shook my head. "I can't die."

She smiled. "I know. You have a man waiting for you back at home." She gave me a wink. "Do you know, I've seen lots of different types of love while on earth, but never one as pure as the one that you and Finn share? He would move heaven and hell for you."

I swallowed back tears. "Jophiel, there is so much that I haven't said to him. This can't be it."

She grabbed my hand. "Walk with me through the field. I'm fading, and there is something that I want to explain to you."

Begrudgingly, I walked beside her.

"Going into the plane with the wendigos was very brave. Some might chastise you and say that it was foolhardy, but the truth is that you were out of options. That dreadful soul, Camaella, will be at the Empowered Academy in twenty-four hours. It doesn't take Haniel or her powers that reside in you to know it would have been a bloodbath. She would have mascaraed everyone there—women, children, even the animals in the woods wouldn't have been safe. This bought you time. Time to gather the troops and prepare for the battle that I believe was always meant to rest on your shoulders."

"Prepare for a battle? I thought I was dying."

She nodded. "Oh, you are." She tilted her head back and took a deep breath. "I'm fading, love. May I give you a gift before I go?"

"Um ... sure?"

She laid her hand at the center of my breasts, her palm warming as the light faded from her eyes. I watched as Jophiel then turned into thousands of colorful butterflies that scattered on the wind, and then I was left alone in the field.

I looked down at my feet and saw a puddle of black oil before I grew incredibly woozy. I hit the grass with a *thud*, and the last thing I noticed was the daisies reaching to me as if they were trying to shade me from the warm sun.

thirty-five

I BLINKED MY EYES OPEN. I was in the small cabin that belonged to Finn back at the Academy of Seraph. I could hear the hum of voices nearby and the sound of a crackling fire.

Had I died? Or was this my happy place to go to before dying?

I tried to lift my limbs, but I couldn't. I was so tired.

A warm head touched my fingers, and I smiled at the wolf that Finn had given me. "Hi, Champ," I squeaked out.

I closed my eyes as the strings around my heart tightened. Emotions that didn't belong to me flooded me. Fear was replaced with happiness, and it all had a huge undercurrent of love. I knew who had just sat on the bed without opening my eyes.

"Finn, am I dead?"

277

A chuckle. "No, Maka, but you almost died … again. What have I told you about leaving me?" He traced circles over my hand with his thumb.

I opened my eyes. Finn hovered over me, his green eyes full of tenderness. He looked so tired. Still handsome but tired. Stubble coated his lower face, and his hair was disheveled like he had spent the night pulling at it.

"I really did almost die, didn't I?"

"We didn't think you would wake. I flew you here, leaving the others to take care of getting everyone else out of the Empowered Academy. This morning, more people showed up than I know what to do with."

I thought back to the woman named Kass and her small child and the old man that was stooped over. "Is everyone out of the dungeons? All the children?"

"Every single one of them. They are currently behind our doors getting fed and warm. Some of the people are with the academy doctor. No one has anything major wrong with them just some small cuts, aches, and pains that needed tended to.

I heard more voices. "Are there people here?"

He smiled. "I had just gotten up to answer the door again. Your friends have gathered out there. I wouldn't let them come in here, because I wanted you to sleep. If you were to have a chance at surviving, you needed to heal. Everyone is upset, other than Hannah. She told us we had nothing to worry about. She's been asleep on my couch for the last few hours."

"Her powers are growing."

He nodded. "And no offense to her, but I needed to see you wake up with my own eyes before I celebrated."

"Not that I didn't enjoy your prowess as a wendigo, but I really enjoy this form better."

His deep chuckle warmed me. "I like this form better, too, but the wendigo did its job of protecting you."

I squeezed his hand. "I can't believe we made it out of there. The last thing I remember is trying to turn the original back, and then everything went dark."

"You would have been able to, but you used up so much of your power before you reached her."

I gave him a confused look. "*Her*? And I didn't change her back?"

"She was killing you. She almost did kill you."

Then it dawned on me. "You killed her?"

He gave me a sad look. "I had to. It was either her or you."

"Who was the original, Finn?" I knew the answer as I put the pieces together, but I needed to hear him say it.

"Jophiel. She was captured a long time ago. They used dark magic to turn her into a beast. They were also using her feathers for the serum. It's what they would use on fully blessed before they took their wings and beheaded them, ceasing the immortal's existence."

"How do you know all this?"

"She came to me one night. Or, actually, she summoned me. She told me that she was tired of being a wendigo.

She said, for years, her brothers and sisters would come to her in dreams, but she stopped all communication not too long ago because it was too depressing watching how they pitied her. Before she refused to talk with them, Haniel told her that you were coming, but in her vision, you died trying to use the Flaming Sword on her. Jophiel begged me to come with you, that if it got to that point, to end her. I did, and when I did, all the blessed were turned back into their original forms and the marked no longer were trapped. They were worried that, if she died in her wendigo form, she would be sent to hell instead of heaven, where some of her brothers and sisters are."

"No. Please tell me she's not in hell."

He shook his head. "Sandalphon showed up here earlier today. He could tell something was off with me. He said that Haniel visited him last night and told him that Jophiel is with them now, waiting on all the other's return. Do you know that you are alive because Jophiel poured some of her powers into you?" He gave me a sad smile. "That's what? Now *nine* archangels you've been blessed by?"

"She saved me," I said. Then I thought of something. My voice shook with emotion, knowing that I would not like the answer to my next question. "Jophiel had mentioned that there would be repercussions if I ended the original's life? What repercussions were there?" My gut churned with despair, and when his green eyes landed on me with such sorrow, I started to cry.

"The original was never meant to be killed. It was the

anchor for all of the other wendigos. All that power that it held inside of it had to go somewhere."

Almost shouting, I said, "What were the repercussions?"

"It will be okay, Maka."

"Will it? Tell me what the price is that you must pay?"

"The beast is still inside of me. It's dark magic swirls inside of me like a parasite gnawing on my insides, wanting to be free. I'm having a hard time not letting the dark magic take over. I have to go for a little while."

"No," I said. I tried to sit up but was too weak.

He rested his palm on me as if he was afraid I would break if I moved.

"You aren't going anywhere. We will work through this together."

"No, Maka. I need to be very clear. If I let the beast out, I don't think I'll be in control of who or what it harms. You, your friends, my people—none of you are safe."

"I'll take the risk."

"I won't." His eyes were hard as granite, and I knew that there was no way of convincing him not to leave me.

My emotions were running heavy, and I was too exhausted to keep my walls up. He quickly picked up my thoughts.

"I would never choose to leave you unless I thought it would save you."

God, I wished I wasn't so weak.

"How do you know this is the right thing? For you...? For us?"

He opened a drawer from the table beside the bed then pulled out a pocket knife. "Before I was turned into a wendigo, I was blessed by the Sandalphon. Most would agree that he is the most powerful of the archangels."

I nodded as he twirled the blade.

"My father is the most powerful of fallen angels. Between the two, it created me—a unique powerhouse that has to constantly make sure I'm keeping on the right side of things—the good side. And it's hard being good." He opened the blade and broke off the knife part as easily as if he was flicking off a light switch. Then, grabbing the handle with one hand, he squeezed. When he opened his hand, the handle of the pocket knife looked like it had been recycled. "Gabriella, I'm just closing my hand on this. I'm not even trying to damage it. What I'm trying to tell you is that I'm not in control of this strength, and I'm sure as hell not in control of the power that is swirling around inside of me. I'm forever changed. This new guy can't stay here. If I do and accidentally hurt you, or someone else, I couldn't live with myself."

"You would never hurt me, Finn."

His green eyes flashed and, just for a moment, I saw the beast that lived inside.

"I have to go. Once Camaella gets to the Empowered Academy and realizes you have lifted the mark of everyone there, killed the headmistress, and the original wendigo is no longer in play, she will have to regroup. You have done something that no one else could have done."

"All of us contributed."

He nodded. "But she doesn't know about the rest. She only knows of you. She will be terrified. This will buy you time to organize a plan of action. You'll run the school while I'm gone."

"I'm not what they need."

"I disagree."

I knew that if he left like this, he would never be back. What he had inside of him was too dark. It was pushing the balance too far to the dark side. I could only gift him with something that I hoped would even out the darkness that now claimed him.

"Come here."

He didn't move.

"You want to leave, fine. But you will kiss me goodbye."

He hesitated for a moment before he leaned forward and pressed his lips to mine. It was an unsatisfactory, chaste kiss.

I rested my hand against his chest, my palm growing warm. This last little push of energy completely drained me. And, as my eyes shut, I heard the man who I loved getting up from the bed.

He would be gone the next time I woke, but he would also be carrying the Flaming Sword with him. The seven that were to carry the sword now had it. Uriel's request was now complete.

I would rest and recover. Then I would pull myself out of this bed and get to work on figuring out a way to stop Camaella from marching into this academy with her demons. And while I worked, I would never stop praying that Finn would conquer that darkness. He would come back to me because, until then, I would never be whole. I would be broken.

CONTINUE THE STORY IN...

broken

special invitation

THREE SPECIAL INVITATIONS

1. I'd love to stay in touch with you and keep you updated about my new books! Join my newsletter to get all the latest information delivered straight to your inbox. Sign up at my website:

WWW.BRANDIELLEDGE.COM

2. Want to hang out with other readers who love my books? Join **BRANDI'S BOOK MAVENS** on Facebook and have fun with us. Oh yeah, I'll be there too!

3. Follow me on Instagram for cool giveaways! You can find me @**BRANDIELLEDGE**.

acknowledgements

EVERY TIME I GET TO this part... the finishing of a book, I feel like I fail. I always forget someone, and for that, I am truly sorry.

Let me start at the top. I have to thank God for loving me even when I'm unworthy. My family for being amazing. Parents that have shown me what the true meaning of strength is. A husband that gets me. Two children who are my greatest achievement and friends who love me enough to help me bury a body if the occasion should ever arise. That sounded a little darker than I intended. Whoops.

We all know that it takes a village to see a book from start to finish. Shout out to the following: Kristin Campbell, my fantastic editor, who is brilliant. My assistant Haley James makes things happen behind the scenes. Molly, oh sweet Molly Phipps, who makes the most beautiful covers. Brook Forshey and Martha Ashe, my amazing beta readers.

Thank you to my author friends who let me bounce ideas off of them, keep me sane, or just let me ramble. Kisses to each of you, Rebecca, Michelle, Sadie, and A.J.

Congratulations to Pam Luna and Ellie-Mae Waters, who got to name a character in Captured. I love Luna and Ezra.

Finally, thank you to all my wonderful readers. You make what I do fun.

about the author

BRANDI ELLEDGE lives in the South, where even the simplest words are at least four syllables.

   She has a husband that she refused to upgrade…because let's face it he is pretty awesome, and two beautiful children that are the light of her life.

Find her online at:

WWW.BRANDIELLEDGE.COM